PRAISE FOR *THE CASE OF WINDY LAKE,*
BOOK ONE IN THE MIGHTY MUSKRATS SERIES:

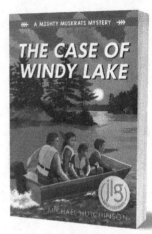

"These tweens are smart, curious, and resourceful."

—JEAN MENDOZA,
AMERICAN INDIANS IN
CHILDREN'S LITERATURE (AICL)

"The Muskrats feel like the kind of real kids that have been missing in children's books for quite some time."

—QUILL & QUIRE

"Chickadee's rez-tech savvy pairs well with her cousin Otter's bushcraft skills, and, along with Atim's brawn and brother Samuel's leadership, the four make a fine team. ...an Indigenous version of the Hardy Boys full of rez humor."

—KIRKUS REVIEWS

"Their makeshift fort in a rusted-out school bus has the appeal of the Boxcar Children's titular boxcar, and in fact there's overall an old-fashioned classic mystery feel along with a look at contemporary rez life in this first installment of a series."

—THE BULLETIN OF THE
CENTER FOR CHILDREN'S BOOKS

"[A] smart and thought-provoking mystery for middle grade readers."

—FOREWORD REVIEWS

THE CASE OF THE MISSING AUNTIE

THE CASE OF THE MISSING AUNTIE

MICHAEL HUTCHINSON

Second Story Press

Library and Archives Canada Cataloguing in Publication

Title: The case of the missing auntie / Michael Hutchinson.
Names: Hutchinson, Michael, 1971- author.
Series: Hutchinson, Michael, 1971- Mighty Muskrats mystery ; bk. 2.
Description: Series statement: A Mighty Muskrats mystery ; book 2
Identifiers: Canadiana 20190185996 | ISBN 9781772601176 (softcover)
  | ISBN 9781772601480 (hardcover)
Classification: LCC PS8615.U827 C367 2020 | DDC jC813/.6—dc23

Edited by Kathryn Cole and Christine Miskonoondinkwe

Fourth printing 2021

Printed and bound in Canada

Second Story Press gratefully acknowledges the support of the Ontario Arts Council and the Canada Council for the Arts for our publishing program. We acknowledge the financial support of the Government of Canada through the Canada Book Fund.

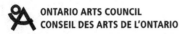

Funded by the Government of Canada
Financé par le gouvernement du Canada

Canadä

Published by
Second Story Press
20 Maud Street, Suite 401
Toronto, Ontario, Canada
M5V 2M5

www.secondstorypress.ca

This book is dedicated to Dorothy and Dick Hutchinson, my mom and dad. I would not be me without them.

It is also dedicated to all my aunties and uncles, who supported and guided me through my crazy years. And to teachers like Cabbie John, who pointed me in a better direction, even as he had his back to the flames.

CHAPTER 1
A Sister Stolen

"Grandpa hasn't seen his little sister since she was taken." As she looked out the back window of the van, Chickadee grappled with the concept of forcefully being pulled from her family. She was also grappling with an idea that was slowly taking shape in her mind.

The Mighty Muskrats were on their way to the city. That morning they had piled into Auntie Maude's vehicle and had spent the past six hours counting license plates, watching for animals (both wild and farmed), and stopping at gas stations to pee and then refuel with chips and pop.

"Taken? Grandpa's little sister? What do you mean?" Atim, seated in the middle, flicked his long hair out of his eyes and scratched his belly. Samuel had the other window, but his nose was buried in a book. Otter was riding shotgun and talking with his aunt.

Auntie Maude looked in the rearview mirror at her niece. Chickadee's long black hair hung over her shoulders. She was wearing her favorite black hoodie and looked back at her auntie in the mirror with bright, empathetic eyes.

"Grandpa told you about his missing sister?" Auntie Maude gave her a quizzical look.

Chickadee nodded. Otter pulled his feet off the dashboard and turned his skinny frame to see his cousin better. His cropped, black hair, button nose, and cute face made him look younger than his eleven years.

Auntie Maude was impressed with Grandpa's trust in her niece. "He doesn't talk about that much. I only learned about it from Uncle Levi."

Chickadee responded to her aunt's reflection. "I asked him what he wanted from the city, and he said all he wanted to know was where they put his baby sister. He said this winter she had called to him in a dream. And then he told me what happened long ago. Short version, I think."

Auntie Maude nodded. "It's a sad story. Your great-grandpa died in an accident at work. Your grandpa was just a teenager. Great-Grandma Doris tried hard to provide for the family. She worked hard, young Grandpa did too, but one day, when Doris came home from work, the police and the government workers were taking her children away. Your grandpa too. They said there were too many kids; said they were too poor."

"But Grandpa has brothers and sisters…" The largest

and most muscled of the Muskrats, Atim, shook his big head slightly, and the fringe of hair over his eyes danced.

His mother looked at him in the mirror. "Yeah, but the older kids got sent to residential school. Eventually, they came back. Grandpa's youngest sister never did. She was scooped."

"Scooped?" Otter gave his aunt a quizzical look.

"Yeah. Started back in the 1950s, lasted until the 80s. The government took thousands of First Nations kids and put them up for adoption or fostering, often without the permission or knowledge of their families. Many of them were sent to other provinces or down to the States or to far-away countries, like New Zealand."

Auntie Maude shook her head sadly. She looked at her sons in the rearview mirror. "I just couldn't imagine someone taking you away from me. What would that do to my heart? It would be broken."

"So, there were residential schools *and* scoops?" Otter winced. His parents had been taken from him by a car accident when he was young. Otter knew the pain of losing his mother and father.

"Yes. Some say that when the residential schools got a bad reputation and were being shut down, the government's next assimilation tactic was the scoops. There were TV and magazine advertisements about First Nations kids for adoption. Isn't that crazy?" Auntie Maude's voice was incredulous.

"So that's what happened to Great-Auntie Charlotte?" Chickadee's voice was filled with disappointment.

"That's her name?" Auntie Maude was impressed again.

Chickadee nodded.

"Wow! Grandpa must really trust you. Even Levi didn't know that! Charlotte." She caught her niece's eye in the mirror.

"I have a Great-Auntie Charlotte!" Otter beamed, but then frowned. "Out there...somewhere."

"I had a friend who was scooped." Auntie Maude's lips tightened as she told the story. "He was a good guy, but confused, you know? He grew up brown, in a white family, in a white town. Said he never fit in. When he came back home, he didn't fit there either. He didn't know how to be an Indian." Aunt Maude scoffed sadly and looked at Otter. "The poor guy never had a home."

"Imagine if your little sister was suddenly gone." Chickadee's voice was filled with sadness at the thought. "You didn't even know if she was being hurt, by...a stranger. No way of finding out if she was okay; if she was with good people."

Atim's mother cringed as she drove.

"Grandpa usually has a reason for telling people things. Maybe this should be the next mission for us Mighty Muskrats," Chickadee ventured.

"The Exhibition Fair is our mission!" Atim squealed

with delight. "It's the best week in the city."

"We got money from Dad and Grandpa, so we have cash to spend," Samuel spoke up over the rim of his book and the sound of the van.

Chickadee was still thinking of her Auntie Charlotte, but an excited Atim hugged her so tightly he squeezed the thought away.

"You guys have never been to the Ex!" Atim beamed. "There's the Cyclone. It spins you in a circle. And there's the Rattler that kinda spins you in a circle while waving you up in the air, like this." Atim's long arm swung back and forth from his elbow.

"Never mind the Exhibition, they've never been to the city! Ever!" Samuel chuckled at his older brother. Atim punched him in the leg. The two boys began to wrestle, rough but playful.

Chickadee and Otter looked at each other and shrugged. It was true, they were almost teenagers, but had never been to the city. Now, they were on their way. The thought filled them both with excitement and fear. On one hand, there were the many stories of city-based adventures told by Atim and Sam and their older cousins. On the other hand, were all the horrors and crimes, and all the young adult movies and TV shows that were pumped out to the remoteness of Windy Lake.

"Stop it!" Atim and Sam's mother's voice boomed in the confines of the van.

The brothers quickly switched from roughhousing, to half-heartedly slapping at each other and being careful not to draw their mother's attention. Atim and Samuel's parents hoped to have some time alone in the small northern town that their father flew out of to go to work. She was dropping them all off at her sister's house to spend the week.

"Wovoka's Wail is playing in the city," Otter said quietly to the windshield. Samuel and Atim were suddenly interested.

"The Wail? That's cool! I love their music." Atim slapped Otter on the shoulder.

"I'd go to that. Is it free?" Samuel shut his book.

Otter shook his head. "I really want to go. They're my favorite band and they're too big to ever come to the rez. Lolly Leach is my favorite guitarist. I have my Exhibition money and then the money I got from working with Uncle Jacob. I was going to ask Harold to take me."

"He'd be fun to go with." Auntie Maude smiled at her nephew. Harold was an older cousin who had lived in the city for years.

"Well! I've seen Wovoka's Wail before." Samuel shrugged.

"Me too!" Atim nodded.

"So, secondary mission!" Samuel smacked his book against his palm. "Get Otter to Wovoka's Wail! Agreed?" The boys all nodded in unison.

Chickadee held up a finger. "What about Auntie Charlotte? There's probably people we could ask about her in the city."

"Okay!" Samuel pinched his chin. "Third-iary mission! Look for Auntie Charlotte."

"Shouldn't that be our first mission?" Chickadee wondered aloud.

"We came to the city to go to the Ex. That's why we got the money," Atim said. "Remember?"

"Sounds like you are all going to be busy." Auntie Maude chuckled.

Samuel suddenly pushed his slim upper body past his brother and then between the front seats to get a better view out the windshield. "We're almost there! This little town is just outside the Perimeter Highway that skirts the city. We should be able to see the buildings soon."

"Put your seat belt on, Sam!" His mother used her elbow to push him back.

"We'll see buildings soon." Samuel continued to scan the skyline from his seat.

"We'll see them when we get past those trees and on that corner." Atim pointed up the highway.

Otter and Chickadee both breathed deeply as the excitement built within them. Chickadee wanted to fly out of the van and stand on the corner up ahead. Otter's foot maintained a steady tap against the floor. The highway rolled on.

The trees they were passing were different from what they were used to at home. Mile after mile of leafy trees spread their green arms and defined field after field of growing crops. The rocks didn't stick out of the earth here. The earth was a fertile black, not the sterile, white mud of the rez. Chickadee looked at the bottom of her pant legs. Sure enough, pale, limestone dust from the Windy Lake First Nation shaded the hem of her black jeans.

"There! See?" Samuel pointed off into the distance. The trees had cleared, and the car was now headed toward a long stretch of fields. Chickadee saw nothing that looked like a city to her.

"Where is it?" Otter was also confused.

Atim leaned forward from his seat in the middle and pointed out some black rectangles in the far distance. "There. See? Those things that look like black pipes sticking up."

Otter squinted. "Really? But they're so small…and there's only a few of them."

Auntie Maude guffawed. "We ain't going to New York, Sunshine!" She gave the steering wheel a slap as she laughed. "Not every city makes the movies, and we're still twenty klicks out."

Otter sat back in his seat and watched the city approach.

Chickadee sighed. She was a bit disappointed. She reminded herself not to have too many expectations.

Samuel leaned over his older brother and touched her arm. "Don't worry, it gets bigger and better."

Atim gave her a nudge. "We'll take care of you."

Chickadee smiled and shrugged. It concerned her more that Atim felt the need to take care of her in the city. She turned back to the window. The city was a little nearer now. It looked like a handful of children's building blocks clustered on the horizon. Chickadee remembered a documentary on the pyramids in Egypt, Asia, and South America. Mankind's first big buildings were piles of big blocks. She was looking forward to seeing the pyramids' great-great-great-grandchildren up close.

CHAPTER 2

Planning and Promises

The Mighty Muskrats' arms were laden with bags as they struggled through the door of their Auntie Sadie's house. A buzz of activity took flight on their arrival. Auntie Sadie stuck her head out from the kitchen and waved down at them with a hand covered in dough and flour.

"You kids are sleeping in the basement! Put your stuff there. Girls on the foldout couch. Boys on the mattresses on the floor. Your cousins already set things up down there." She ducked back into the kitchen.

Auntie Maude went up the few steps that led to the first floor to greet her sister in the kitchen. Auntie Sadie and her husband had moved to the city with their three children to find work. She became a nurse, he worked for a company that had him flying out to a work camp for three weeks of every month. Their oldest son, Harold, was in his first year of college.

The Muskrats and their younger cousins, Nitanis and David, dragged the bags over the field of shoes, boots, and moccasins just inside the entrance. They stumbled down the staircase to the basement. Patches of rug and carpet were strategically placed over the concrete floor. An ancient foldout couch was disemboweled in front of a TV and showed signs of being used the night before.

"You can sleep with me, Chickadee!" Nitanis squealed as she dropped the bag she had been carrying and leapt onto the bed. Her shoulder-length, dark brown hair took flight as she jumped.

"We had other cousins here last night. We always have lots of company during the week of the Ex." David was a little older and a little more thoughtful than his sister. His big, dark brown eyes matched his hair color. He dropped his load along the wall.

Chickadee sat cross-legged on the foldout. Nitanis snuggled up to her.

Samuel curled up in an armchair and reopened his book. "Who was here last night?" he asked as he found his last page.

"Cousins Troy, Doyle, Simon, and Joel," David explained. "Doyle said they only get to eat McDonald's when they come to the city. And they only come to the city when they see the dentist."

Nitanis took over the story. "Troy said he's not sure

he's ever really tasted McDonald's because his mouth is always so frozen."

David smiled at his cousins. "And Doyle once bit his tongue so hard, blood came out. He thought he was chewing his burger!"

They all laughed.

"Gross!" Atim snickered. "Hey ya! You guys can try McDonald's."

"I had a cold burger once." Chickadee shrugged. "Mom brought it from the city."

Otter had found his Auntie Sadie's guitar and began to tinker with the strings. "Do they taste better than the hamburgers from the Arena?"

Atim snorted. "The Windy Lake Arena? Yeah. Those things are terrible. In the city, you can find cooks who don't think freezer burn is a spice."

"So far, the city has been different from what I expected—and the same," Chickadee said thoughtfully, as she put her long, straight black hair in a ponytail. Otter nodded in agreement.

"What do you mean, Chickie?" Sam's eyes left his book to peer at his cousin.

"I thought there would be more people on the sidewalks, I guess. And it's not all tall buildings. There are a lot of little ones. They're all different, but all the same too. It's like walking through bush you don't know, all the trees are different, but all the trees look the same."

Otter chimed in. "I thought we'd see nothing but people on the sidewalks too. And it seems to go McDonald's, TechMart, Pizza Palace, Food Boy, McDonald's, TechMart, Pizza Palace, Food Boy…. Is that pattern repeated over and over through the whole city?"

"Just different neighborhoods, I guess. We were driving in along the main road." Atim gave a half-shrug as he explained.

"And it's busy downtown, when everyone is at work, but it gets quiet in most places when everyone goes home in the evenings. That's why there's a rush hour." Samuel kept reading as he spoke.

"Rush hour?" Otter sounded skeptical.

"The busy time when all the roads are full of people going home. It's the only time Mommy swears," Nitanis cautioned.

"We're going to have to figure out who we talk to about Auntie Charlotte," Chickadee said thoughtfully.

"We have to figure out how we're going to get to the Ex," Atim countered.

"Going to the fair isn't a case. Neither is getting Otter's tickets. Finding Auntie Charlotte is what we should focus on." Chickadee looked around at the other Muskrats for support.

Atim groaned. "I haven't been in the city for ages, I just want to have some fun."

"We'll go to the Ex! But we also have a missing auntie

to look for. This is for Grandpa, right?" Chickadee looked at Otter for support. Otter shrugged and nodded.

"Sam?" Chickadee pulled Sam's book down for a moment.

He waved his hand and nodded.

"Okay!" Atim threw up his hands in resignation. "The Muskrats are on the Case of the Missing Auntie. Satisfied?"

Chickadee smiled and nodded.

"Mom told us about you finding that old man up at the lake." Nitanis tugged on Chickadee's arm.

"He was an archeologist!" David rolled his eyes at his little sister.

"Well…we didn't really find him," Otter said. "We just figured out that everyone was looking in the wrong place."

The correction didn't seem to put a dent in Nitanis's admiration for her older cousins.

"Still pretty cool." David smiled at Atim.

Atim shrugged. "Was Ol' Relic that found him, really. Walked him out on the end of his shotgun." He laughed out loud.

"Ol' Relic wasn't on the news. But you were," Sam chimed in.

"We saw you on APTN too. Mom made us watch the news that night." David's voice was full of wonder. "I said, 'Those are my cousins,' when you came on."

"It was so cool!" Nitanis squealed.

"Well, we have a new case now, and we've got to figure out how we're going to find Grandpa's little sister," Chickadee said seriously.

"Can I help?" Nitanis asked.

"Me too!" David beamed.

Otter patted him on the head affectionately and nodded.

"Well, my brain needs food to work. Do you guys have any food?" Atim rubbed his belly and feigned weakness.

"We do! We have snacks." Nitanis jumped off the bed and headed upstairs as she spoke. David raced his sister to the kitchen.

"That was kind of mean." Chickadee and Otter laughed at Atim.

"I was just giving us a chance to talk, you know, about the case." Atim sounded defensive.

"Mm-hmm." Chickadee shook her head at him.

"There has to be some kind of government office somewhere," Sam suggested.

"Could you do a search on the computer, Chickadee?" Otter rubbed his cousin's shoulder as he asked her.

"Sure. I bet Auntie Sadie has a computer around here somewhere."

"Once we have that, we'll have a starting point." Sam smiled.

"In the meantime, it shouldn't take us long to get Otter's tickets." Once Atim decided he was going to do something, he was like a dog with a bone. He just couldn't stop chewing at it.

Nitanis appeared with a huge smile and arms full of chip bags.

"Snack time!" David followed his sister carrying a selection of drink boxes in his stretched-out T-shirt. The Muskrats thanked their younger cousins and quickly doled out the goodies.

Samuel finally put down his reading. "We should go to the ticket booth in the mall tomorrow. We can get Otter's tickets there."

"The mall?" Chickadee's mind filled with a flood of TV images.

Nitanis squeezed her arm. "I love the mall. There is so much stuff there."

"Star Stores has a lot of cool video games, toys, and stuff. It's the best store at the mall," David advised.

Atim looked for the TV remote as he spoke. "The mall is cool. We can get the tickets there. If the concert's not sold out...."

Otter stopped strumming Auntie Sadie's guitar, concerned. "What do you mean, 'sold out?'"

The oldest Muskrat shook his head and sighed. "The stadium is only so big. There're only so many seats."

"So, I might not get in?" Otter was surprised at how sad the thought made him. His cousins could hear the worry in his voice. Nitanis and David frowned in sympathy.

Atim patted Otter on the shoulder. "Don't worry, cuz, we'll get you the tickets. If they're all sold, we'll figure something out."

Samuel pursed his lips. "I wouldn't promise. The concert is in just a couple of days."

Atim straightened himself out and pointed to the sky. "I promise I'll get you tickets, Otter. There's always other ways in the city. It's who you know."

Samuel laughed. "You don't know nobody!"

Atim threw a pillow at his brother. Samuel deflected, but the fluffy projectile hit David, who threw it back at Atim. Chickadee and Nitanis grabbed the pillows off the bed and launched them in the air.

CHAPTER 3
An Old Friend Found

"It's easy. Just get on, drop your change in the slot, and take a seat," Samuel assured Chickadee and Otter as the bus pulled up. The doors opened, Samuel stepped on, slowly dropped his coins into the cache, and walked toward the back. Otter followed but dropped his coins in a rush. Two of them jammed in the slot. Those that followed bounced off and hit the floor.

Giggling, Atim and Chickadee joined in the scramble for the fleeing bus fare. Chickadee looked up to see the bus driver watching them disapprovingly. She smiled up at him.

Eventually, they gathered all the wayward coins and joined Samuel at the tail of the almost-empty bus.

"Welcome to my big, orange limousine." Sam stretched his arms out across the back of the seat. Chickadee slipped into a seat by a window. Atim, the oldest and tallest

Muskrat, smacked the ceiling of the bus before he sat down beside her. Otter slid in beside Samuel.

"It won't take us long to get there. This bus goes directly downtown." Atim rubbed his belly. "I can't wait to hit the food court."

Samuel snickered at his brother. "I like the food court because of all the different kinds of people there. It's not only cultures, but rich and poor people too. Downtown is where all the office crowd is, but it's also where homeless people and panhandlers hang out."

Atim thumped his chest. "And freaks.... You gotta be tough in the city."

The other Muskrats rolled their eyes.

Chickadee was watching the city slide by. The repetition of the suburbs had given way to a layer of older buildings as they passed through the Old Town neighborhood. The office buildings of City Center were newer and had stores and restaurants filling their lower floors. Chickadee saw a man sitting on the sidewalk. The bus moved past so fast she didn't get a chance to get a good look. She wondered if she had just seen her first homeless person.

Eventually, they were downtown, and Chickadee was delighted to see the big signs, neon adverts, and colorful posters plastered everywhere. The bus pulled up to a stop in front of the mall. The Muskrats tumbled out into a press of people.

"Stay together!" Atim shouted at his smaller cousins. It didn't take them long to get out of the crowd around the bus stop and into the mall. Atim quickly led them to the food court and found them a table. As they settled, he took off to line up for his favorite fast food. The other Muskrats chuckled at their perpetually hungry cousin.

Chickadee had a moment to look around her. She was surprised at the sheer variety of people. The food court was the most multi-cultural place she had ever been to. Groups of old men from every corner of the globe were chatting and laughing amongst themselves. She was grateful to see a group of First Nations Elders also had their place. Chickadee was comforted to find brown faces in the city, even if they belonged to people she didn't know.

Samuel noticed her gaze. "Lots of First Nations from up north come down here to shop and, this week, go to the Ex." Sam hitched up the hand-me-down jeans on his slim frame.

Suddenly, Atim's voice broke through the hubbub. "Hey guys! Look who I found!"

The cousins turned to see Atim, with a tray piled with food, and a boy who had moved from Windy Lake a few years before. Brett had been a leader back on the rez. He was from an older age group, so the Muskrats had always looked up to him.

Chickadee's face turned red as she saw Brett. It wasn't until after he left their community that she realized she had a crush on him.

"Hey, gang!" Brett's clothes looked brand new and fashionable. "I haven't seen you guys for, like, two summers." He hugged Otter and Samuel. Atim sat down and began to eat.

Brett slid into the seat across from Chickadee. Otter was across from Atim and stole the occasional fry from his plate.

"How do you like the city, Brett?" Samuel was pinching his chin.

"S'alright." Brett stretched his legs out into the aisle. "Started out hangin', like, at the mall more, once I was old enough not to need my parents along."

"Atim is our guardian." Samuel chuckled as he pointed his thumb at his brother.

"Ouv nemer meen no naiff!" Atim said with a mouth full of food. The others laughed.

"I said…" he found a final morsel hidden in his cheek, "…you've never been so safe."

Choking and laughing, Atim wiped his chin as he finished chewing.

Otter feigned seriousness and slapped Atim on the back. "Don't forget to breathe, cousin."

"I missed you guys. We laughed so much back home." Brett chuckled.

"Who you hangin' with now?" Samuel stole a fry from his brother's tray.

"I don't know. Just some guys who live in the neighborhood." Brett rubbed the back of his neck and looked at the floor. "To be honest, not really sure they're friends."

"Well, we're your friends," Chickadee said and meant it.

"No doubt about that." Atim was almost finished his tray of food.

"For now!" Brett laughed, but his eyes were serious. "Everyone forgets about me once they get back home."

"I won't," Chickadee declared.

Her cousins were quiet for a moment and then broke out in giggles.

"*Eeewww*, so deep!" Atim teased. Samuel hid a big smile behind his hand.

Chickadee scowled at the boys. She picked up Atim's dirty napkin from the tray, scrunched it into a ball, and threw it at him. Then she launched a half-hearted kick at Samuel's leg. On the outside she laughed and accepted the teasing, but inside she was mad at herself for being so open and was a little upset that the other Muskrats had belittled her feelings. She wasn't sure what these feelings were, but she did know her cousins had bruised them.

When she looked back at Brett, he seemed to be absorbed with his phone.

"I'm sorry, guys. I gotta go. My friends just texted me, they need me to…run an errand." Brett got up quickly and put his phone in his pocket.

"Really?" Chickadee's voice held a touch of disappointment.

"Your friends have you doing stuff for them?" Otter smirked as he said it.

"Yeah, just stuff. I'm the new guy, so…" Brett shrugged.

"Auntie Sadie gave me a phone to use while I'm babysitting in the big city." Atim waved an older cell phone back and forth. "Give me your number. We're probably going to the Ex tomorrow. I'll text you and let you know if we change plans." Atim stood and slapped Brett on the shoulder. As Brett gave him the number, he punched it into the borrowed phone.

When Atim was done, Brett looked around the group. "I'll see you all again before you go."

Chickadee and the boys nodded.

There was a moment of silence.

"Sheesh. Get out of here!" Samuel laughed. Otter and Atim each gave Brett one last slap on an arm, and then he turned to leave. The Muskrats watched him walk away.

"You guys gonna eat?!" Atim suddenly broke the silence. "What are you going to share with me?"

The other Muskrats groaned.

After everyone had their fill of food-court fare, the Muskrats made their way to the ticket booth.

"This is going to be amazing!" Otter couldn't think of wanting anything more. He had followed the career of Wovoka's Wail's guitarist, Lolly Leach, and was really touched by their lyrics, which mixed their traditional Paiute language and English.

"When they played the city on National Aboriginal Day, they were so loud!" Atim laughed and held his ears.

"I can't wait to see them. I hope Harold will be into it." Otter put his hands together as if to pray.

When they got to the front of the line, Otter asked Samuel to speak to the lady behind the glass.

"Two tickets for Wovoka's Wail, please." Samuel laid Otter's cash out on the counter.

The lady pursed her lips and then her fingernails clicked against the keyboard.

"That's what I figured." She leaned toward the glass. "Wovoka's Wail was sold out just two days after it was announced. There may be some contests that still have tickets, but you'll have a tough time finding some now. Of course, there are still VIP seats, but they're twenty dollars more a ticket. Sorry."

Samuel gave Otter a look of disappointment. Otter's jaw dropped and then shut. He looked at the floor, crushed. He didn't have enough money for VIP tickets.

The lady noticed. "You know, what usually happens for these big shows, is that the stadium guys don't really know how large the stage is until they show up. So sometimes there can be some regular tickets released once they know how much space the show really needs. You never know… there's still a chance."

Samuel turned back to the lady at the counter. "Thank you anyway. We'll figure something out."

"Good luck," the lady said sincerely. Then she looked beyond Samuel at the person behind him in line and yelled, "Next!"

The Mighty Muskrats walked a short distance and then clustered around Otter. They put their hands on his shoulders.

"That's too bad, Otter." Chickadee rubbed his back.

"It's okay." Otter's voice was dripping disappointment, but he was trying to soldier on.

"This isn't the end…" Atim was determined. "We'll get you those tickets, I promise."

Otter looked at him, hopefully.

"Atim, you shouldn't…" Samuel warned and shook his head.

"I promise!" Atim stated loudly.

Samuel shrugged, but it was obvious he wanted to say more.

Atim slapped Otter on the back. "Don't worry," he whispered in his ear.

"I'll help as much as I can." Samuel was realistic about their chances but didn't want to let Otter down either.

CHAPTER 4

Desperate Plans, Desperate Measures

"We might as well go to the fair," Otter announced the next day at the breakfast table. He awoke, resigned never to see Wovoka's Wail. The Muskrats had emerged from the darkness of the basement and now sat in the brightly lit kitchen.

"There are other ways to get tickets. We can do it!" Atim was adamant as he poured syrup on his Insta-waffles.

"I don't want us all to miss the Exhibition Fair just because of me." Otter shook his head and then smiled. "I'm sure I'll see the Wail when they're old and wrinkled like the bands the aunties go see."

"I don't think they've changed the records at the gas station on Windy Lake since my mom was a teenager." Chickadee laughed.

"The aunties! They might know a way to get tickets that we don't!" Atim slapped his fist into the palm of his hand.

After they had eaten, Atim found Auntie Sadie in her bedroom getting ready for work.

"Auntie Sadie, you wouldn't know how to get tickets when a concert is already sold out, would you?" Atim leaned against the doorframe.

His aunt laughed. "That's a tall order."

"I know, but this is Otter's first trip to the city, and I really want to be able to make sure he gets to the Wovoka's Wail concert."

"Well…actually, under my credit card, I'm a preferred customer, so I would be first in line for any new tickets that come up. I'd need to use my card to buy the tickets, so you'd have to give me the money first." Auntie Sadie sat down in front of her makeup table and started painting her face.

"What does that mean?" Atim felt weird watching his aunt apply makeup.

"It means, you have to promise to give me the money for the tickets. Then I could buy any new ones that might come up or get VIP tickets, if you have enough money for that."

"Really? That would be great!" Atim was ecstatic. "Thank you, Auntie!"

"It's a long shot, but you have to give me the money first. I'm willing to help, if you've got the cash."

"It's another chance. We'll get that extra money."

"Well, it's nice you're trying to do this for Otter. He

hasn't had it easy since his parents went on their final journey."

Atim gave his aunt a kiss on top of her head.

She smiled at him in the mirror. "Listen, there's a bowl full of change at the top of the stairs. If you guys need money for food and the bus, you can take it out of there, so you don't have to spend your Exhibition and concert money."

"That's awesome, Auntie. I'm going to go tell Otter we still have a chance." Atim bounded out of her bedroom.

His aunt called down the hall after him. "If you kids want a ride downtown, hurry up and be ready when I go."

Atim bounced back to the dining room to tell Otter and the others the news, and an hour later, the Muskrats were outside the mall, waving good-bye to their aunt.

"So where are we going to get that extra money, smart guy?" Samuel sounded skeptical as he pinched his chin.

"I don't know. I'd chip in my Ex money, so Otter could go to the concert." Atim raised his eyebrows waiting for others to follow suit.

"No way!" Otter shook his head. "No way am I going to be the reason that Chickadee doesn't get to go to the Exhibition Fair."

"I thought the Ex was mission number one," Samuel said.

"It was, but it'll be there all week. We can go any day." Atim flicked the hair out of his eyes. "But imagine if Otter could go to the Wail on his first visit to the city!"

"And what about Auntie Charlotte?" Chickadee was a bit chagrined that she too had forgotten about their Grandpa's request, but that didn't stop her from giving her cousins heck.

"Just a few more hours on Otter's quest, and then we'll get to the others. I'll figure something out," Atim insisted. Samuel raised his eyebrows expecting a response from Chickadee. She shook her head but didn't push further.

Disappointed in herself and her cousins, Chickadee began to walk slower, looking in the store windows, but only seeing memories from when her Elder had first told her about his missing little sister.

★

"She was always a happy girl," Grandpa said. "She had that sweet innocence kids have when they're young."

Chickadee made tea while her grandpa spoke. She filled the kettle with water and placed it on the stove.

"I remember once, when I was supposed to have been babysitting her, she disappeared. Maybe that was a sign...." He shook his head. "We all searched the house—everywhere. We searched the yard. We searched the sheds. You know where she was?" Grandpa chuckled.

Chickadee shook her head.

"She was in the garden." He slapped his knee. "She was sitting in the garden, in the big leaves, so we couldn't see her. But Charlotte could see us, and she had been sitting there watching us, as she was eating peas.

"We laughed hard when we found her because we had all been so scared. She was very precious to us." Grandpa got quiet for a moment. His chin tightened as he tried to keep his emotions in check. He looked at Chickadee with watery eyes. "Sometimes, when everyone thinks you're lost, you're really where you're supposed to be. Sometimes, when everyone thinks you're right where you're supposed to be, you're really lost." He smiled sadly and wiped his eyes.

"You never told me about your little sister before, Grandpa." Chickadee poured hot water over a tea bag in the cup. She put the kettle back and then placed the cup in front of her Elder.

"I haven't dreamed of her in a long time." He took a sip. "But I did recently. I saw her, and she was far away but she was saying good-bye because she was going farther still."

Grandpa had always asked them about their dreams. Dreams could be an important source of information. He had told them they were important tools for better understanding your own heart and mind...and that sometimes dreams served as a link to different things that were greater than yourself. He had told them that back in traditional times, warriors could not hunt a bear until the bear came to them in a dream and told them it was okay.

"Do you think something happened to her?" Chickadee's voice held her concern.

"It was like hearing her speak to me through a mile-long pipe, while she was walking away from the other end. Something is changing for her." Grandpa nodded. "She is thinking of us."

"Why now?" Chickadee wiped the kitchen counter as she spoke.

"I don't know, little one. I don't know."

★

"We have to make Auntie Charlotte our number one case." Chickadee planted her feet in the middle of the mall hallway.

"What?" Atim looked at her quizzically as all the boys turned.

"You guys have to promise me we'll look for our missing auntie. You have to *promise* me we'll look for Charlotte."

The boys knew Chickadee well enough to know when she was drawing a line. There wasn't much point in fighting about it. Sam and Otter shrugged and looked at Atim.

"Fine. I promise!" Atim sighed and stared at the ceiling.

"I'm cool with it," Sam assured Chickadee.

Otter smiled and nodded.

"But we're going to spend today getting someone to help us with those tickets." Atim was also adamant.

The boys looked at Chickadee. She couldn't hold her serious face for long with her cousins looking at her so expectantly.

"Anything for my boys!" Chickadee's smile beamed out from her freckled cheeks.

"We're supposed to meet Brett at the food court again." Atim looked at the text message on his borrowed phone. He started walking into the mall, and the remaining Muskrats followed.

Chickadee found herself thinking of Brett. He had always been able to make her feel better when they were friends back on the rez. He looked a lot different now with his city clothes, but she was sure he was the same guy on the inside.

Chickadee studied the stores as they made their way through the crowded hallways. *So much stuff.* She wondered if it all sold. *What happens to the stuff no one wants?* Her thoughts were interrupted as they got to the food court. Samuel pointed out an empty table that could fit four.

"Okay. I'll meet you there. I'm getting something to eat." Atim flicked his hair out of his eyes and took off. The others made their way to the table and sat down. One by one they got their own food and returned.

The Muskrats didn't have to wait long before Brett found them.

"So, the Wail tickets were sold out, but now we might have a new way of getting them. We just have to make a little more cash than we have," Atim explained to their city-wise friend.

"When I need extra cash, I take what I got and, like, I go to The Crystal Palace and play pool." Brett looked around the group. "There's a few people there who play pool for cash. I usually win, if I stick to playing the posers."

"Posers?" Otter was sorting the recyclables from the trash on his tray.

"Like, guys who try to be something they're not. Lots of guys at The Crystal Palace think they're good at pool, but they ain't." Brett laughed.

"And you are?" Chickadee smiled up at Brett.

"Of course! I bet we're all a little better than most kids in the city. They didn't have the old pool table from Windy Lake to practice on."

The whole group chuckled at the thought of the ancient plywood building that housed the Windy Lake Youth Centre. The pool table was the highlight of the experience. Brett had won many of the numerous tournaments the Youth Centre planned in order to keep the young people of Windy Lake occupied.

"But are we old enough to get into The Crystal Palace?" Sam pinched his chin. The idea of exploring a new place was intriguing to him.

"It's an arcade and pool hall, not a bar," Brett said with

a smirk. "Look, if you don't want to double your money, like, that's fine. It was just an idea."

"Double our money?" Atim sounded eager.

"I figure we could double your money, depending on who is there." Brett sounded confident.

"A bet is always a risk," Samuel said, wincing at the thought of losing their Ex funds and feeling that they were about to do something they shouldn't.

"Let's just check it out." Atim was willing to follow any path that could lead to tickets.

Sam looked at Chickadee. She was certain Brett wouldn't take them somewhere they'd get hurt. She assented with a shrug.

Sam looked at Otter.

"Wouldn't hurt to check it out." Otter was also interested in seeing something new.

Brett was pleased. "That's great. How much money we got?"

"Well...my dad gave us all five dollars and Grandpa gave us all five dollars, so we have ten dollars each." Atim was adding on his fingers. "Times four...that's forty bucks!"

"Forty bucks. Like, that's it?" Brett sounded disappointed.

"Well, that's our money for the Exhibition Fair. Otter has a hundred dollars from working with Uncle Jacob. That's his money for the Wail tickets, but since the regular tickets are sold out, we need more cash for the VIP tickets," Atim blurted out.

Otter was a little chagrined as Brett slapped him on the shoulder and called him "Big Spender."

"So, a hundred and forty bucks." Brett smacked his hands together and smiled.

"Maybe we should think about this," Samuel said.

"Yeah, everyone should be able to decide, if they want to chip in." Chickadee was looking at Otter's face.

"I don't want to bet my ticket money," Otter said quietly and shook his head.

"You don't have to, but I'll chip in my Exhibition money to give it a shot." Chickadee touched Otter's arm, nodded to him, and then looked at Brett seriously.

"Me too," Samuel said.

"Okay. Forty bucks. I guess, like, it's a start." Brett sounded disappointed.

"Okay. Now that that's settled, where is this Crystal Palace place?" Samuel was excited to go.

★

They walked through the business area and into a thin slice of stores and restaurants on the edge of a residential area. This neighborhood was a little dirtier than the groomed streets of downtown.

Brett led them toward a discount store. Along its side

wall was the door that led down to The Crystal Palace. The doorway was surrounded by garishly painted signs that proclaimed it an all-ages arcade and pool hall. Brightly colored placards also declared fresh-cut fries, pool leagues, and cappuccinos as selling features. The door of The Crystal Palace creaked loudly as it opened. The sound was quickly followed by the smell of fried food and old carpet.

"This is it?" Chickadee looked concerned as she peered down the dark stairwell. Samuel also looked a little worried.

"It's fine. Let's go." Brett thundered down the steps. Atim and Otter followed quickly behind.

After a shared glance, Chickadee and Samuel made their way down to the arcade.

CHAPTER 5

The Crystal Palace

The Crystal Palace was a mixture of deep shadows, colorful neon, and arcade lights. It smelled like the ghosts of greasy burgers and spilled pop. A sit-down counter filled the wall in front of them. A grizzled old man behind it gave them a once-over and then returned to his chores. The main room was a field of green and red as pool and snooker tables were spread from wall to wall. To the left, a smaller area was partially blocked off, inside blinked an array of video and pinball games. A palisade of pool sticks lined the outside walls. A scattering of players focused on their games. The smack and click of pool balls colliding kept a random tempo.

The Mighty Muskrats stood in a bunch right inside the door.

Brett seemed to know the place well. "Let me ask around if there's anyone that wants a game." He walked up to a group of teenagers and began to speak with them.

Chickadee reassured herself that Brett wouldn't take them somewhere dangerous, but this place made her nervous. Atim walked the distance to the counter, grabbed a stool at the closest end, and began to study the large menu plastered on the wall. Samuel, Otter, and Chickadee slowly meandered closer to the largest Muskrat.

Brett returned and told them the game was on.

"I'll play their best guy a game for, like, all the money." Brett started walking back to the table and waved for the Muskrats to follow.

"One game and all our money? Brett better be on the ball." Samuel's voice was hopeful.

"He'll kick their butts. Remember what he said? Brett knows what he's doing." Atim nodded confidently.

"Thank you for doing this." Otter put a hand on Chickadee's shoulder and looked around at the group.

"It's okay. Let's just get out of here as fast as we can." Chickadee had agreement from all.

Brett was picking out a pool cue when the Muskrats walked over. His opponent was hefty, shaggy, and was about seventeen. His denim vest and jeans didn't look like they'd been washed in days. The big teen's friend was thin with clipped dark hair. He was dressed better, in a matching tracksuit and expensive running shoes. They both watched the Muskrats with smirks.

"So, you little kids up for a game?" The large teen smiled down at them. "It's an easy game. There's fifteen balls, a table with a pocket at each corner, and pockets in the middle on either side. I use the white ball to knock the other balls into the pockets, and after I sink seven balls, I sink the eight ball. And then I win. You got that, children?"

The Muskrats smiled tight smiles at the condescending teen.

"We're just here to watch. Brett's playin'." Atim tried to sound casual as he shook the hair from his face.

"Well, I'm sorry for taking your money. Just put it over there." Their opponent guffawed and pointed at a stand-up table between their two groups. Chickadee collected the money from her cousins, placed it on the table, and then sat down.

The Muskrats scowled at the big bully. Brett walked up to the table with his chosen pool cue and grabbed a cube of chalk. He rubbed the chalk on the tip of his stick to make it less likely to slip against the ball when it made contact.

"Go get him, Brett." Chickadee clapped her hands a couple of times.

"You got this." Atim slapped Brett on the shoulder as he went by.

"Get 'im, Brett," Otter said.

Brett looked nervous.

"Your break." The teenager waved his hand at the table.

Brett took the white ball and placed it opposite the triangle of racked pool balls. He leaned forward and rested his left hand on the table. Brett balanced the front half of his cue in the valley between his thumb and fingers, so that the tip was pointed directly at the white ball. His right hand pulled and pushed the cue back and forth as he eyed the shot. Suddenly, his arm tightened, and, with a sharp, quick jab of the stick, he sent the white ball crashing into the formation of striped and solid colored orbs.

The Muskrats cheered as two spheres went in, one solid and one striped. Brett sunk another stripe before he caught a bad bounce and the targeted ball rolled away from the desired pocket.

"Too bad, so sad." The teenager arrogantly walked around the table before choosing a solid-colored ball to hit. He slammed the green ball into a corner pocket and then followed that up with the yellow. His third shot caught a purple ball at a wrong angle and sent it bouncing off the soft bumper along the edge of the table and away from the intended pocket. The teen swore loudly and smacked his cue against the table.

Brett was one ball behind as he aimed at a red-and-white striped sphere. It shot into the back of the pocket like a bullet. The white ball continued to bounce around the table, pushing other balls out of its super-charged way. Eventually, it came to rest against the bumper edge of the table. Four other balls now blocked the paths to most of the table.

"Poop!" Brett looked concerned.

"What's up? You're tied now." Atim moved from his spot along the wall and stood closer to Brett to consult.

"I should have, like, paid more attention to my next shot." Brett studied the table. "Good pool players always shoot so the white ball is, like, set up to for their next shot. I forgot to do that and now the white ball is right up against the rail."

Atim pointed to a purple-and-white striped ball, a few inches from the bumper, but closer to the far corner pocket. "You could try that."

Brett shook his head. "Yeah, but like, then where?"

"No coaching!" The big teenager laughed, hit his buddy on the shoulder, and turned his back on them.

Atim returned to the tall round table where Chickadee and Otter were watching the game.

Brett studied the scattering of balls for another moment and cued up the target that Atim picked.

The Muskrats held their breaths. Brett aimed at the white ball below its center, so the cue put backspin into the white ball's course across the table. It hit the purple-and-white ball, and then slowed and stopped, rather than rolling forward normally. Brett now had an easier angle to get a different ball down the side pocket. The purple-and-white ball plunked into the pocket.

"Backspin!" Brett smiled. The Muskrats all exhaled.

After Brett sank another ball, his opponent began to watch the game more closely.

Chickadee noticed and quietly said to her cousins, "Big guy's getting nervous."

The teenager tried to hide his concern with belittling. "That was luck." He took a long pull on the straw of his soft drink.

Brett seemed more confident. But he hit his last stripe a little too hard and it rattled between the corners of the pocket. "Like...argghh!" Brett leaned against his cue and rubbed his forehead with his other hand.

"Shake it off, Brett! You're up by four!" Atim cheered.

"Just one more and then the eight ball, Brett. No problem." Chickadee smiled.

Otter gave Brett a brave look and lifted his fist in the air. Brett smiled back at all of them and then watched the big guy shoot.

"Got to clean this up," Brett's opponent growled at his friend.

After walking around chalking his cue, the denim-clad teen bent over the table and sank a solid red ball. With a serious expression, he sank two more balls, and then his face relaxed a bit as he studied the table for his next shot.

"You're right behind him, boss," the other teen encouraged. "Two more then the eight ball."

Brett's opponent nodded and circled the table. "I'll put

these kids to bed right now." He snapped a blue ball into a corner pocket and tied up the game. He leaned back and smiled at the Muskrats. "Your hero boy is going down."

Chickadee raised her eyebrows at him and then looked back at the game.

The teenager lined up the next shot and then teasingly regarded the Muskrats as he sent the ball toward a pocket. But the ball swung wide and bounced slightly off the rail. The bully looked at where his ball landed and swore loudly. He stood and smacked his pool cue against the table.

Brett sighed. They both had to sink one more before they started shooting at the final ball. Sinking the black eight ball wins the game. The Muskrats cheered on their player.

Brett stood quickly and shot at his last ball. It rattled in the pocket. The Muskrats held their breaths, but then the bouncing stopped. The sphere balanced on the rim. Slowly, it tipped over the edge. It landed with a click as it hit the other balls at the bottom of the pocket.

The kids let out a loud cheer. But the white ball kept rolling. It hit the bumper gently and came to rest behind his opponent's last solid ball.

"Ha! Hooked yourself," the teenager shouted. "You have to hit that eight or you've lost."

Brett looked ill. It was a rule, if you're on the black ball, you must, at least, hit it with each shot. With the white ball hugging his opponent's ball, and the table edge just an inch or two behind, it was unlikely that Brett could find an angle that would bring the white ball in contact with the black one.

The only way he could hope not to hit the solid ball first was to shoot toward the edge. He looked at the eight, back at the white, and then back at the eight. He picked an angle, changed it and then picked another. Brett hit the white ball with medium force. It bounced off the rail, past the last solid, and then wandered across the table to hit the far rail. It stopped six inches from the black ball.

The big teenager jumped and fist punched the air. The Muskrats gasped and then they all shared disappointed glances. Brett looked at the floor, his cue stick resting horizontal across the table.

"Get my money." The laughing winner pointed at the stack of cash. His friend got up and swiped the winnings.

"Now…I'm going to leave you sad, sad kids alone." He frowned like a clown as he looked at the Muskrats. "It was our table, so allow us to pay for it…with your money." The big teen laughed. He walked over to Brett and whispered something in his ear. Brett's shoulders slouched farther when he heard his opponent's words. With his buddy in tow, the big teen wandered over to the man at the counter.

The Muskrats gathered around Brett.

"It's okay, Brett." Chickadee squeezed his arm.

Otter slapped him on the back.

"You almost had it, man." Sam softly punched Brett in the shoulder.

Atim had been hard hit by the loss. He looked Brett in the eyes and shook his head.

"You had it, Brett!" Atim shook his head. "We'll figure something out."

Brett looked around the circle of friends. "I'm sorry. I'm sorry, I messed up. I thought I had him!"

"Ahh, well. I didn't need to go to the Exhibition anyway." Chickadee's laugh was tinged with disappointment.

"C'mon, let's get out of this hole!" Samuel smiled. He looked over at the collection of pinball and video games as he turned to leave.

The youth from Windy Lake left The Crystal Palace and walked back to the mall.

CHAPTER 6

Backspin Blues

Brett said few words as they all walked back to the business district. The Muskrats did their best to cheer him up about the loss. They all agreed that the Exhibition Fair was an annual event and they could all go another year. Brett didn't respond. A cloud of disappointment surrounded their little cluster as they made their way to the food court.

They were quiet as they slid into seats that were bolted to the floor. Atim leaned heavily on the table. "I'm so sad, I'm not even hungry."

"Really?" Samuel looked incredulous.

"Well, having no money helps." Atim's smile had a touch of chagrin.

"Hey!" Brett said angrily. "I tried."

Atim looked shocked. "I didn't mean to make you feel bad, Brett. Just sayin'," he stammered, sincerely.

"Well, you guys still have a hundred bucks. Why don't you spend that?" Brett still sounded defensive.

Samuel leaned in. "That's Otter's money. Don't feel bad about losing, Brett. We knew the risks and we have to accept the results."

"We're not mad at you." Chickadee touched Brett's arm. Otter nodded.

The Muskrats attempts to make Brett feel better seemed to do the opposite.

He stood up angrily.

"Maybe you should forget the tickets and just, like, buy some new clothes. O-M-G! You look like you just, like, walked off the rez." Brett didn't look any of them in the eye.

"Brett?" Chickadee tried to draw his eye.

He shied away, then he looked down at her. "You're just a bunch of kids…."

Chickadee's heart was punctured.

Brett watched the look on her face change. "You're not old enough to be walking around the city." He turned to leave but yelled over his shoulder, "Maybe you should just go back to your auntie's!"

Incredulous, the Muskrats watched him walk away.

"What was that about?" Samuel blinked.

"He's upset that he lost," Atim said.

"He's upset he let us down, probably," Otter added.

"Could be. Or…I don't know, something else."

Chickadee tried to sound like an adult, but she felt an ache on the inside.

"Well…" Atim said slyly, "we really should get back to Auntie's."

"What are we going to tell her about our Ex money?" Chickadee raised her eyebrows at the boys.

"What are we going to tell Auntie? Why do we need to tell her anything?" Atim tried to sound casual.

"We just lost all our money!" Chickadee wailed.

"It's only forty bucks," Atim said.

Chickadee threw her hands up, leaned back against her seat, and crossed her arms.

"Well, we'll keep it quiet for now. If we have to tell her, we will. But if we don't, we won't," Samuel said, trying to be a peacemaker.

Chickadee glanced at Otter. He had other places to look. She shook her head. "And what about Great-Auntie Charlotte?"

The boys were silent.

Eventually, Samuel stood up. "Let's just head back to Auntie Sadie's now. We'll figure things out in the morning."

"Sounds good." Atim pushed himself aloft using the table and chair. He then let his legs down to the floor. Otter and Chickadee followed the brothers.

Nobody said a word on the bus ride back to their Auntie Sadie's.

CHAPTER 7

Chickadee Takes Flight

Chickadee ran. Fingers of pine needles clawed her face. Thorns and brambles entangled her legs as she crashed through the trees. Was it behind her? Was she running toward it? Her leg muscles screamed as they thrust her forward. Where was she going? Fear tightened her chest. A ghostly fog filtered through the evergreens.

The bush was thick. Chickadee tried to protect her face as the branches slapped her like angry hands. She staggered as the ground dipped and rose again. Almost on her knees, Chickadee caught herself and resumed running.

"I'm here!"

Who was that? Did she hear that? She gauged her fear. What was she running from? Was it closer? Farther?

"I need your help!"

That wasn't a thought. Someone was there with her. She stopped. Her breath was ragged.

Chickadee dared to whisper, "Where are you? Are you lost?"

A wave of sadness hit her. She was so alone. Was that her emotion or someone else's? Something was left unfinished.

"I am here! Help me."

The sorrow was overwhelming. It was a weight Chickadee carried as she picked through the bush and fog toward the voice.

"I am coming!" She gasped under the load of despair. "I want to help you!"

As the heartfelt desire to help surged within her, Chickadee was suddenly pulled forward through the bush, the trees fading behind her.

In a blur, she was at the edge of a small dell. The sorrow and loneliness had intensified. She looked across the tiny clearing within the evergreen witnesses. The mist seemed to suck the color from the air. Then the vapor parted, and something slowly emerged—a small girl. Her skin was pale, strands of long, black hair obscured her face, a gray smock hung from thin shoulders.

Chickadee's fear rose inside her. She wanted to run, but the girl's hand beckoned.

"Who are..." Chickadee stepped back.

"My circle is broken. Please, don't be afraid. Help me!"

The girl faded into the fog.

★

Chickadee woke with a start. Her heart felt like it pumped sadness with every beat. The pain ebbed as she caught her breath and her heartbeat slowed. When she was feeling normal again, she laid her head back on the pillow and hoped she would remember the dream in the morning.

She didn't.

★

Hours later, Chickadee awoke to sunlight shining through the basement windows. She looked around at the piles of clothes and bags, and the furniture pushed against the walls. On the floor, Otter and Samuel slept head-to-foot on a queen-sized mattress. Close by, Atim was snoring loudly on a smaller air mattress.

Chickadee watched her cousins sleeping for a moment. She sighed, shook her head, and quietly got out of bed. After brushing her teeth in the downstairs bathroom, she dressed and went upstairs. Looking out the windows by the back-door landing, she saw that the sun had just pulled its bottom over the horizon. She climbed the last few steps to the first floor, past the kitchen, and down the hallway that led away from the living room. Her aunt had told her there was a study with a computer on the other side of the bathroom.

Chickadee had never seen so much carpet and her feet were delighted by its softness. She knew her Auntie Sadie and her uncle were not rich, but they both had careers, and their house was nicer than any back at Windy Lake.

Chickadee found the computer and turned it on. Once it whirred to life, she began to search the Internet for information on adoptions. The search engine came up with the provincial adoption agency. Opening that website, Chickadee began to search the archives. After a few minutes, she realized that older records had not been uploaded to the web. Her auntie Charlotte's records were too far back to access online. The website advised the searcher to visit the Provincial Archive building for hard copies of the files. It also recommended that an appointment be made to access a staff member. Chickadee wrote down the address and began to search for the bus number that would take her there. Armed with new information, she headed back through the still-quiet house.

As she passed the door to the kitchen, she saw her cousin Harold eating breakfast at the kitchen table. Chickadee smiled. "Hey, Freaky."

Harold looked over the cereal box in front of him. "Hey, little cuz. It's so nice to see you." He waved at her happily. "I've been so busy with work and school that I'm hardly here. I heard you were in. We'll have go to the mall or something."

Chickadee jogged over and gave him a hug.

"Grab a bowl and some cereal." He pushed the box at her. "Let's talk."

Over their breakfast bowls, the two gossiped about family and Windy Lake for a while. Harold was older than the Muskrats and he had babysat Chickadee and his younger cousins many times. He knew them well. After a time, their conversation moved on from just family, friends, and back home.

"So, what have you thought of the city so far?" Harold asked.

"It's big, but then…it's full of little caves, small places where people are closed off. I don't know…." Chickadee scowled.

"I know. It's got so much, but then it's so empty too," Harold said. "For me, it's good, because of the way I am." He flipped his hair with a flick of his wrist. "I'm a little loud and I like to be different, so the city is better for that than small-town Windy Lake."

They both laughed.

"But then, coming from the rez, I know there is a different life. I know what the bush sounds like. And everything in the city is so…city-centered. Why do we have a mine polluting Windy Lake? Because it feeds the city. Everyone wants to get more of everything so that their lives are easier. Time moves faster here it seems." Harold picked up the cereal box and offered Chickadee a second helping, but she shook her head.

"The craziest part is…" Harold continued, "city people don't seem to know there is a different life out there.

It's like the city mouse killed the country mouse and forgot he ever existed. Our people can get lost in the city."

"Harold, did you know about Auntie Charlotte?" Chickadee drank the last of the cereal milk directly from the bowl and then joined her cousin as he put his dishes in the dishwasher.

"Not until last night when my mom told me. Pretty interesting. And pretty cool that Grandpa trusted you with it." Harold closed the dishwasher.

"Well, I was on the computer, and the provincial website says I should go check out the archives and ask for hard copies if I want to find out more. What's a hard copy?"

Harold laughed. "Just a printed copy. Maybe the files are stored on microfilm or something. I don't know. But do you have to go down there?"

"Yeah." Chickadee sighed and shook her head.

"What's the problem, little one?" Harold gently placed his hand on her shoulder.

"If this was Windy Lake, I'd just walk over."

"Well, Atim has to get up…eventually. He's a growing…bonehead, you know." Harold giggled.

"They're all boneheads!" Chickadee said, exasperated. She told Harold that the boys had been more interested in getting tickets for Wovoka's Wail than finding Auntie Charlotte. She was just tired of boys.

"Girls mature faster than boys, most times. I feel for

you." Harold squeezed her shoulder. "You know, the archives are on the way to the university. It's just one bus there. You cross the street and catch the same bus to come back home. If I go there with you, do you think you could make it home?"

Chickadee nodded enthusiastically.

"Okay, but you better be able to. You're underage, and Mom and the aunties would kill me if you got lost. Still…I think you can do it."

"I'll be able to babysit other kids in a year…-*ish*. And I've taken the bus before. No problem," Chickadee assured him.

"Okay. Get your stuff." Harold smiled and they both got ready to go.

CHAPTER 8

A View of the City

"So, when you said you were tired of boys, it seemed like you were speaking about more than your cousins." Harold smiled at Chickadee.

Her cheeks suddenly took on a reddish glow. She looked out the bus window and watched the buildings go by.

Harold poked further. "Must have been someone you knew from before. You've only been in town for a few days."

"Brett!" Chickadee sighed. "He seems different. I don't know, I would've trusted him with anything before, but now...I'm not sure."

"Brett? Musky's little brother?" Harold scrunched his face as he thought.

"Yeah. We've hung out with him since we've been here, and yesterday he took us to this place called The Crystal Palace."

"The Crystal Palace? That place is a dive! He shouldn't have taken you there."

Chickadee wondered if she should tell her older cousin the whole story, but she'd promised the other Muskrats she would keep quiet about losing their Exhibition money.

"Anyway, that's why I wonder about Brett now." She looked at her older cousin and shrugged.

Harold gazed out the window for a while before he spoke. "It's funny. There are more rules and less rules all at the same time—more options and more competition and more pressure. It makes people...change."

Chickadee felt he wanted to say more, so she kept quiet.

"You know, I'm different here too. It sounds silly, but my city friends call me McKenzie. They say it suits me more than Harold. And...I think it does too."

"McKenzie does suit you," Chickadee said softly.

"Doesn't it?" Harold snapped his fingers. "In the city, I can be...more myself. More me!" He threw up his hands and laughed. "But at the same time, I feel I'm more myself when I'm home in Windy Lake. It's weird...back home, there's a...it's like a play. Everyone has an assigned role that was given to them as they grew up. It's hard to leave those roles, even though you may be a different person in high school than you were as a kid, and later, maybe a different kind of adult altogether. But then, in the city, when those roles are taken away, some people get lost in all the options."

"Do you think that's what is happening to Brett?"

"I don't know. Maybe not. Brett's older brother, Musky, hangs out with some pretty sketchy people. And his family has always been poor."

"What does poor have to do with it?"

Harold scoffed. "You pay more money, you get better seats for the concert, better lawyers for better justice. A better neighborhood often means better health care. Nobody questions it. In a lot of ways, it's harder to be poor in the city than it is in Windy Lake."

Chickadee thought about all that she had seen in the urban environment. So much stuff just hanging in the malls, picking up change off the bus floor, homeless people mixed with business people.

Harold continued as though he just remembered something. "You know, that's one of the reasons I volunteer."

"Volunteer? To do what?"

"Just help out mostly. I volunteer for a couple of groups, but my favorite is the Indigenous Arts and Music Board. We put on street fests and concerts in poor neighborhoods. I was supposed to work one later this week, but Mom wants me to take you guys to the Exhibition."

"Sorry." Chickadee was upset that she couldn't tell her cousin the truth about their Exhibition money.

"No worries, there's a bunch I can still go to." Harold shrugged and then pointed toward the front of the bus. "Hey, we're coming up on your stop." He suddenly went into older-cousin mode. "Okay. Remember to take a look around when you get off the bus. Remember what you see because you'll have to find it again. As soon as you get off, look across the street, find the bus stop that will get you back to my mom's house."

"You sound like Grandpa...." Chickadee deepened her voice and tried to sound like her Elder. "Make sure you always look back along the trail you've walked, so you know what the way home looks like."

"Well, Grandpa always has good advice. And looking back at where you've walked is good to do in the city as well as in the bush."

They shared a laugh. An older lady in front of them turned around to look. This just made them giggle more, but they tried hard to suppress it.

"Pull the stop dinger." Harold gave his little cousin a push. Still chuckling, Chickadee stood, pulled the bell, and walked toward the door as the bus slowed down. Harold waved at her enthusiastically. Chickadee smiled and gave a little wave back. She was grateful for the talk they'd had.

CHAPTER 9

Into the Stone Sphinx

As soon as the bus left, Chickadee took a look around. Across the street was a big park. At its far end, an old building stood, looking very important, behind a small squad of statues. Official-looking buildings rimmed the road on the other side of the park. There wasn't a structure in sight that resembled anything on the Windy Lake First Nation. She smiled as she remembered the mining company's dirty warehouse. It was the biggest building in her traditional territory. She took a moment to find the bus stop across the street where she'd take the bus back to Auntie Sadie's.

When she turned around, she was immediately struck by the structure behind her. It was constructed out of huge blocks of limestone that were just a bit taller than she was. Chickadee's gaze floated upward. This building looked like a great-great-granddaughter of the pyramids.

It wasn't as tall as the buildings of the business area, but it seemed like it was from a different age. On each floor above the first, rows of little square windows broke up the limestone face. The wings of the building spread forward from the center. As she walked toward the front doors, she felt like she was walking between the paws of a giant, resting sphinx.

The inside seemed bigger than the outside. The tall cathedral roof along the front facade allowed the light from the little square windows to shine into each floor of offices. The inner parts of the building were crafted with much smaller blocks of limestone. Every sound seemed sharp. Chickadee could hear a lady's high heels click against the hard floor.

She counted seven floors above the one she stood on. Chickadee imagined all the people stacked up in this building, working at desks, clicking on computers, answering phones. More people than all of Windy Lake, maybe.

Tellers were helping people or working on computers behind the big counter about thirty steps in front of her. But closer, and off to one side, was a small information desk. A young, blonde woman smiled expectantly at Chickadee. When their eyes met, the lady asked if she needed directions.

"I'm looking for information on my Great-Aunt Charlotte." Chickadee tried to sound businesslike.

"Well, I think we can help with that. What kind of information were you looking for?"

"She was adopted out in the Sixties Scoop, and I'm trying to find her." Chickadee approached the desk.

The government worker made a face. "Uh…maybe I spoke too soon. Give me a moment." The lady picked up a phone and spoke to someone about Chickadee's request.

When she hung up, she pointed to the big counter. "Someone will meet you over there to discuss your request."

Chickadee smiled and thanked the young woman. She thought it was funny that all the information the lady behind the Information Desk had was that she should go to the great big counter with all the people sitting behind it.

As Chickadee approached the counter, an older woman with long, auburn hair waved at her from the far end. Once she got Chickadee's attention, she stood and waited with her hand on her hip. Her face wasn't very welcoming but it changed a little as the woman realized how young Chickadee was.

"How can I help you, young lady?" The woman didn't smile, but she didn't seem annoyed either.

"My great-auntie Charlotte was taken by the government when she was around seven. I'm trying to find her now." Chickadee continued with her businesslike attitude.

"How old would she be now?" The woman raised an eyebrow.

"Uh…" Chickadee remembered back to the details her grandpa had told her. Auntie Charlotte would have been around six or eight when she was taken some time in the late 1950s. Grandpa figured 1958. Chickadee quickly did some math, but realized, without a birth date, she didn't know for sure. "Around her late 60s, I guess. It was a long time ago. Do you have records that go back that far?"

"We do, but not those kinds. Adoption records are only available from the post-adoption registry, which is not far away." She looked down at Chickadee as though remembering she was a young person. "It is in a different building."

Chickadee listened to the directions the lady gave her and took the little piece of paper she had scribbled a map on. She left in a fog. She knew this search wasn't going to be easy, but even so, she was disappointed to hit this first obstacle. She thought of her grandpa. He'd tell her that she had some sign now, some clue as to what her search involved, where it was heading. This was just the first track on the trail.

She looked at the map in her hand. She held it to match the landscape before her. She'd have to cross the park and walk two streets down to find the building she was looking for. Three blocks, tops, and then she would walk the three blocks back here to catch the bus. No problem.

CHAPTER 10

The Boys Bounce

The boys woke after Samuel moved in his sleep and kicked Otter in the face. After some groaning and complaining, Otter and Samuel sat up and rubbed their eyes. Only then did they notice the empty spot on the pull-out couch.

"Where's Chickadee?" Otter leaned back to look past the staircase and into the laundry room.

"I don't know." Samuel checked out her bags. "Looks like her hoodie is gone. Maybe she's gone out already."

Atim sat up. "Do you think she'd say anything to Auntie Sadie about yesterday?"

The boys all looked at each other.

Samuel shook his head. "I doubt it. She would have said something last night."

"Well…" Atim yawned and rubbed his face, "…maybe. Let's get up and out of the house. I can send Auntie Sadie a text or something later."

The boys agreed they'd go out for breakfast. They dressed quickly, tried to tame their bedheads using water from the basement bathroom sink, and slunk out the back door.

Once they were on the bus, Atim texted Auntie Sadie and told her that they were going to the mall.

A few minutes later, she replied, "Did you guys eat? It's almost lunchtime."

He texted back, "We're eating out."

She returned, "LOL. You guys need to eat some real food. Stay safe and take care of each other."

"Looks like we're good to go." Atim smiled and leaned back in the seat.

"Did you hear anything from Brett?" Samuel's brow furrowed.

"Not yet. Do you think we will?" Atim looked skeptical.

"I have no hard feelings." Otter shrugged. "I can understand why he was upset yesterday."

"Text him," Samuel said to his brother.

Atim texted their friend and told him they'd be at the mall.

After the bus stopped, the boys made their way to the food court. They had taken some extra change from the bowl Auntie Sadie had offered. They had enough money for some fries and a Coke. They agreed to share. Samuel and Otter knew it was doubtful all the fries would get back to the table if Atim went to get them, so Sam volunteered to go up to the counter.

"Fries and a Coke that we'll have to share!" Atim rubbed his aching belly as he waited. "I'm hungry, I'm in the city, and now I'm eating like I'm back at the House-teraunt."

"With that much money back home, we'd be sharing a burger too," Otter chimed in. "With spicy freezer burn."

Atim tried to stay annoyed, but Otter's joke made him giggle.

When Samuel came back, he had the fries, soda, and three paper cups.

"Very fancy," Atim said as he poured out the pop equally.

"That's what I figured." Samuel chuckled. "Now I don't have to taste your backwash."

The borrowed phone vibrated. Atim read aloud a text from Brett. "Sorry for being a loser last night. I know a guy who has tickets for sale. Meet me at back door of the mall."

"What do you think?" Atim's eyes moved from the phone to Sam and then Otter.

"If Brett knows a guy, we may be able to cross the tickets off our list," Samuel said.

Otter waggled his head from side-to-side, considering, and then he nodded as a small smile crossed his face.

The boys cleaned their table and dumped the recycling

and garbage. They dodged adults as they filtered through the mall to the back doors.

In the bright, summer sunlight outside, they all squinted after leaving the sparse lighting of the mall. Eventually, as their eyes adjusted, Otter picked out Brett waiting near a taxi stand. A taller teen stood with him.

"Hey, Brett," Samuel said as they strode up.

"Hey, kids." Brett turned and smiled at the Muskrats.

Brett calling them *kids* caused all the boys to slow down.

"I got a friend here." Brett indicated the freckled teenager with his red hair in a groomed mess, and clothes that looked freshly picked from the mall. "He has some tickets to Wovoka's Wail for sale, but you have to go to his house to get them."

"Okaaayyy." Atim sounded more than a little skeptical.

"How do we get there?" Samuel pinched his chin.

Brett presented the first taxi at the stand as though he were on a game show. "Step right up, young man. Our chauffeur will drive us to, like, the castle in question." Brett opened the back door.

The driver yelled out the open door. "I can only take four passengers."

"Gentlemen, one of you will have to stay." Brett motioned for his friend to get in the back. After the teen got in, Brett said, "Probably best if Atim stays, he's the biggest and will be able to fend for himself while we're gone."

Atim nodded his assent and agreed to wait for them there. Samuel and Otter walked toward the cab. Otter slipped into the back seat with Brett and his friend. Samuel sat in the passenger seat beside the driver.

CHAPTER 11

Bullies and Betrayal

The cabbie was tall, thin, and hadn't shaved in a few days. His long salt-and-pepper hair hung around his shoulders. It was mostly salt. He smelled like an ashtray but smiled at Samuel with intelligent eyes and a long face full of smile lines. "Where we off to, young man?"

"We're heading to the apartment building at the corner of Home and William," the redhead shouted from the back.

"Really?" The grizzled cabbie looked in the rearview mirror.

The redhead nodded.

"Okay, you're the boss." The driver turned on the meter and the car began to roll.

"How long you know Brett?" Samuel asked the teenager.

The redhead grunted and didn't stop looking out the window.

"He doesn't, like, talk much," Brett said. "We'll be there soon."

The taxi continued into a run-down area of the city. Apartment buildings and rowhouses were squeezed between the occasional industrial buildings. A thin drizzle began to distort the picture outside the windows of the cab. Eventually, they pulled up beside an old, brick apartment block that seemed to be crumbling right in front of them.

"Here we are." Brett motioned for the redhead to get out. "One of you pay."

"But what about the money for the tickets?" Samuel asked.

Brett looked over his shoulder as he got out of the taxi. "Just pay for it, we'll take, like, whatever is left."

The cousins looked at each other. Otter gave Samuel ten dollars to give to the cabbie and then left the car.

"You sure you boys want to stop here?" the cabbie asked, looking at the apartment building.

"This is where my friend says his buddy lives," Samuel told him.

"Are you sure he's your friend?" The gruff driver smiled, but Samuel could see he was serious.

"We'll be okay." Sam tried to sound confident as he handed the man the cash.

"If you say so." The cabbie slipped the bills into a cigar box and shoved it back under his seat. "Sounds like you're going to check it out, no matter what I say." He chuckled, and his face broke out into a well-used smile.

Doubts began to creep into Sam's mind, but he knew that he would still follow Brett into the building. The mixture of apprehension and certainty almost made his brain tickle.

"Yeah. But…thanks for caring." Samuel liked the old guy immediately.

"No problem. Glad to spread a little warning here and there." The cabbie smiled as Samuel got out and closed the door. The taxi, slowly, pulled away.

Samuel caught up to the boys as they reached the front door of the building. His worry grew the closer they got. The building looked deserted. The windows were filthy and broken.

The redhead pulled the door open. The hinges complained loudly, obviously forced to do a job they hadn't been asked to do in a while. With a nod of his head, he indicated that Samuel and Otter should enter.

"You live here?" Sam asked the teenager. He looked back but didn't answer.

"Upstairs, third floor," Brett said. Samuel regarded his friend from Windy Lake. Brett pointed with his chin at the open door.

Otter and Sam stepped inside. Now it was obvious

the building was abandoned. The floor was a haze of dust. Dozens of footsteps betrayed their age as they headed off into the building's crumbling depths. Wallpaper hung in jagged tears from the walls. Samuel stopped. "It looks like nobody has lived here for years."

"Makes for cheap rent." The redhead laughed and gave Samuel a little shove toward the stairwell. "I live on the third floor."

Sam and Otter hesitated.

"Go!" Brett barked angrily.

They started up the stairs and almost immediately heard footsteps descending. When they arrived at the first landing, they were met by those coming down. It was the denim-clad teenager from The Crystal Palace and his track-suited buddy.

"Hey children, we meet again," the hefty teenager drawled.

Samuel and Otter turned to Brett, who ignored their gaze as he stood behind the redheaded teen.

"If you had coughed up all your cash for Brett's little scam yesterday, none of us would be here!" The big bully laughed and blocked any escape upward.

The redhead stepped forward and slammed Otter against the wall.

At the same time, the larger bully grabbed Samuel by the arm and forced him up against the bannister.

"Who's got the rest of the cash?" The big teen spit in

Sam's face. He leaned his full weight on Samuel's torso, making it hard for him to breathe. Sam tried to push the bigger teen back but couldn't move him.

The redhead gave Otter a quick jab to the lower ribs. The wind left Otter's lungs. As he bent over, trying to catch his breath, the redhead dug in his jean pockets for the money.

Suddenly, a pounding thundered up the staircase, and Brett went flying down the steps. The old cabbie stepped onto the stairwell landing. The redhead aimed a punch at the old man, but the driver stepped around it and tossed the freckled teenager down the stairs after Brett.

He grabbed Samuel's arm and pulled him away from the denim-clad bully. Then he grabbed Otter's arm and began running down the staircase with the boys in tow. Down they stumbled, jumping over the groaning hoodlums at the bottom, and out the open door of the abandoned apartments.

Only then did the cabbie let go of them. "Get in my cab!" he shouted as he waited by the door for any of the thieves to come out. When none dared to show a nose out the door, he loped back to the taxi and got in. He laughed as he put the car in drive and sped away.

CHAPTER 12
Cabbie John

"I can't believe it!" Otter held his side and rocked back-and-forth in the backseat. "I can't believe he lied to us!"

"Believe it!" Samuel said, shaking with anger. "Right from the beginning it was a scam."

"Nobody has used that building in ages. I thought something was up when they wanted to take you there. You boys should be more careful. Where are you from? Up north?" the cabbie asked as he navigated the thickening traffic.

"How did you know?" Otter gingerly inspected his aching ribs.

"Ahh. You kids from up north come down here and have no idea what the city is like. You just assume every-one will take care of you, like in your small town back home." The grizzled man shook his head.

"Thank you for what you did." Samuel nodded in

appreciation at the man. "One of those guys was a friend of ours. Or…we *thought* he was a friend."

"Well, I couldn't let those meatheads hurt you." He looked at Sam. "They call me Cabbie John." He stuck out a hand.

"I'm Sam and this is Otter." Samuel shook the cabbie's long-fingered paw. "And we can't believe Brett took us to those…meatheads."

"Don't judge your friend too harshly. People do a lot of stupid things out of desperation. I always say, a guy has got to eat. If a young man can't feed his family from what happens in the daylight, he'll get what he needs from the night." The driver sounded like a professor.

"Where are we going?" Samuel asked looking back at his cousin. Otter was leaning against the seat. He held his stomach.

"I was going to drive you back to the mall, but I'm willing to drive you home." Cabbie John watched Otter in the mirror. "You should get him home, Sam. A strong punch can damage things on the inside. Especially, if he wasn't expecting it."

"We can't go back without Atim." Samuel had no idea how Auntie Sadie would react to a badly bruised Otter and no Chickadee. There was no way he was going to show up without Atim.

"We haven't been gone that long; he could still be at the back of the mall." Otter spoke through gritted teeth.

Cabbie John drove the boys to where he had picked them up, and sure enough, Atim was still waiting there. After Atim heard the story, and freaked out a little, Cabbie John drove them back to Auntie Sadie's. He shot a concerned look at Otter in the backseat.

When they arrived, Atim helped Otter out of the car and into the house.

Samuel said good-bye to the man who had saved them. "Sorry, I don't have any money to give you. But we really appreciate all that you did for us."

"Ahh." The long-haired, old man looked at his watch. "I can still catch the tail end of rush hour…if I want to." Cabbie John gave him a mischievous smile. "But I have to ask. You knew there was something up with your friend Brett and his buddy. Why did you go with them?"

"I don't know. Deep down, I guess, I knew. But I thought it was worth it to find out if Brett had really… betrayed us." Samuel looked at his hands.

"Well, courage isn't always smart." Cabbie John chuckled. "It was instinct that told you something was wrong. You should trust that more."

Samuel smiled, opened his door, and stepped out. He closed the door and looked back through the window. "I'll think about that."

"Just be careful out there, Sam." Cabbie John grinned as he drove away.

Samuel entered the house only to hear his older cousin

Harold berating the other boys in the living room. Samuel stepped in quickly to support his brother and cousin.

"How did this happen?" Harold demanded. Atim's mouth fell open but no answer came out. Harold had Otter lying down on the couch and was pressing his fingers against Otter's abdomen. Harold's face was filled with concern. "Does this hurt?"

"It just aches. But there's no pain from you just pushing." Otter shook his head while he covered his eyes with a hand.

"It's probably just bruised. You're lucky I came home before class. How did this happen?" Harold asked again. With his angry cousin's attention on Sam, Atim moved and stood farther away.

"Some boys jumped us for our money. They saw we had cash, and then…when we were outside the mall, they grabbed me and Otter, and took our money, mostly Otter's." Samuel didn't know why he summed up the situation without mentioning Brett.

"Well you're lucky to be alive." Harold took one last look at Otter's bruises and then pulled down his shirt. "You guys can't go to the mall downtown anymore. It's too dangerous." He shook his head. Otter sat up and swung his feet to the floor. Harold sat beside him and rubbed his back.

Samuel was going to argue, but then he just shrugged. "We're broke now anyway."

"Where's Chickadee?" Harold looked worried.

"She wasn't downstairs when we woke up," Atim blurted out.

"She left with me, but she should have been home by now!" Harold suddenly stood up. "Where the heck is she? It's starting to rain. I'm calling the police!" Harold was upset. He grabbed a phone and started dialing.

The boys didn't know what to do.

Just then the back door burst open. Everyone ran to see who was there.

A disgruntled Chickadee stared back at them from under her dripping, black hoodie. Her long, raven hair hung in tangled strands. Her blue jeans were rain-soaked. Chickadee's eyes were red and she tried to blink away tears. She had no desire to let the boys see her cry, so she stomped her way downstairs, took off her wet clothes, and went to bed.

CHAPTER 13

Crush Hour

When Chickadee arrived at the building, she was shocked by its difference from the stone wonder of the main archives. These post-adoption archive offices were functionally bland and made of gray brick, black glass, and brown plastic. The nice old guard at the door gave her the proper floor and office number.

An open door led to a small counter and a two-chair waiting area. Chickadee walked up and rang the bell. In a few moments, a young woman smiled down at her. "Thank you for coming to the registry. My name is Janice. Can I help you?"

Chickadee explained her quest to the young woman. After giving Chickadee a form to fill out, the woman called her supervisor.

"I'm Mrs. Yenna. Can we help you?" The older woman peered over the rim of her glasses. Somehow, Chickadee knew Mrs. Yenna didn't appreciate children. She told her story for the third time that day, but she wasn't expecting much from Mrs. Yenna.

The older woman punched Auntie Charlotte's full name into the computer. Something came up on the screen, which she read for a long time. Chickadee waited patiently, but eventually asked, "Find anything?"

"Nothing I can share. Without a date of birth, her name will only get us so far. I'll get Janice working on this, but we'll need that date of birth before we can do anything. Sorry." Mrs. Yenna walked back to her desk in the area behind the counter.

Janice returned and helped Chickadee fill out the form as much as possible with the information they had. Janice assured Chickadee she would do what she could.

Chickadee left the building, got her bearings, and walked back to the bus stop. She was disappointed. The supervisor obviously knew more than she would say. As she waited, she paced, thinking about her frustrating afternoon. Lost in her own thoughts, she didn't realize how many people had come to wait at the stop. It wasn't until a bus pulled up that she realized a small crowd had formed. She looked up at the bus and saw that it was the route she wanted and got in line with all the others. Her change tinkled into the cache.

This wasn't like the few other times she had ridden the bus. A host of faces stared at her as she walked down the aisle, and she thought of what Brett had said about her clothes. All these city people probably knew that Chickadee was from a reserve. People looked away as she walked by them. She wanted a seat, but she was almost at the back, and there was no place to sit down. Several people were already standing. Chickadee turned around, but another bunch of people now blocked her view of the front. The bus started with a lurch. Chickadee stumbled, took a step, grabbed the passenger bar, and hung on.

The bus soon stopped again. More people came aboard. The group between her and the door moved back. A middle-aged man, in a dirty yellow vest and a hard hat, walked down the aisle toward her. Chickadee squeezed her way toward the people behind her. A young woman, with a backpack over her shoulders and a large purse swung over an arm, texted on her phone with her thumb. Chickadee got as close as she dared, then stopped. She turned around; the large construction worker was right there. She could smell his work sweat. Chickadee looked over her shoulder and stepped back toward the girl. The girl scowled. The bus lunged forward. Chickadee half-stumbled but did a better job of catching herself.

In a blink, the bus stopped again. She couldn't believe more people were allowed on. Everyone pushed back. The little space Chickadee had shrunk even more. She had never been this close to strangers before. There were so many people too close to her. Chickadee looked down. A seated couple looked back. She tried to see out the windows, but a sputtering rainfall had started. It had mixed with the road dust and smudged the windows. The bus was now a beige box.

Chickadee turned. The young woman glared. She looked forward. The construction worker's arm held onto the overhead bar, his hairy armpit emitting odor. Chickadee couldn't breathe. She closed her eyes. She could feel the people around her as they reacted to the motion of the bus. A prickly heat raced up her neck and face. Chickadee felt like an unbreakable shell was growing around her. It was too tight for her chest to expand. She had to get off! Chickadee urged her feet to stay still. But unstoppable fear rose inside her. Her feet began to push her forward. The construction worker swore as she shoved past him.

"Sorry, sorry. Oh, I need to get out! Sorry." Chickadee held back tears, pushing her way through. She tried to gently slip by an old woman holding on tightly as the bus wriggled through traffic. Through the crush of people, Chickadee could make out the doors. She struggled toward them, but the other riders were oblivious to her concern. With an irrational terror pushing her forward, Chickadee forced her way through. The bus slowed. Chickadee pushed on the door handles. They refused to open. She pushed as hard as she could. A green light flashed above. The doors gave way quickly, and Chickadee tumbled out into the mud on the street.

The people she had just pushed past began to step off the bus.

A young man with a skateboard looked down at her from the bus steps. "Stupid Indian. Go back to the rez." He stepped over Chickadee and onto the sidewalk.

Chickadee got up quickly and stepped up onto the curb, brushing the dirt off her clothes. The busload of people pulled away from the scene of her embarrassment. Chickadee looked around. The neighborhood was kind of old. A colorful Italian restaurant stood across the street. On her side, the bus had just passed a gas station before it had stopped. Other shops and restaurants stretched off into the soggy distance. No matter where she looked, nothing was familiar. This was just another faceless corner in a huge city. And she had spent the last of her bus fare.

CHAPTER 14

Heading in One Direction

"So were you freaked out when you had to figure out how to get home?" Sam shoved a spoonful of sugary cereal in his mouth and eagerly leaned toward Chickadee at the breakfast table. The Muskrats were alone in the house with their auntie at work and the little kids at day care.

Chickadee poured her cereal and waited for Atim to finish with the milk. She had a new attitude today. Yes, she got kind of lost and walked over an hour in the rain, but she had figured out how to get home, and she had pushed their case forward. Last night, she was still mad at the boys for not taking their missing auntie more seriously. She went to bed as soon as she got home without saying a word to any of them. This morning, she decided she was going to find Auntie Charlotte, whether the boys helped her or not.

"I followed the bus stops and walked home. No biggie." Chickadee shrugged.

"You looked pretty wet when you came in last night," Atim remarked. "Maybe even like you had been crying."

Chickadee rolled her eyes at her cousin. "I was mad at myself for getting off the bus in the wrong place. That was all."

"That was it?" Otter arched his eyebrow.

"Well, I actually fell off the bus." Chickadee giggled picturing herself in her panic. "But then, there was some guy who called me a 'stupid Indian' and told me to go back to the rez."

Little drops of milk shot-gunned across the table as Atim coughed out some of his cereal.

"You're kidding me!" He was angry.

Chickadee shrugged. "No. I tripped coming off the bus, so I was lying there in the mud. And then he shaded me as he got off." Chickadee quietly wondered if she'd be able to handle it the next time she was close to so many strangers. She knew she wouldn't even have to face that again if she stayed in Windy Lake.

"If I was there, I would have hit the guy." Atim shook his head angrily and then slammed his fist into his palm.

"Settle down, big guy. No reason to get upset about what some idiot racist says." Sam lightly slapped his brother on the shoulder.

Chickadee was thoughtful as she spoke. "It was different from when someone calls me an Indian at home. I didn't know the guy, not even a little, but he hated me just for who my family was. It was...sharper for some reason. Made me angry..."

"I think that's natural." Otter gave Chickadee a half-hug. "Sorry you had to go through that, Chickie."

"I'm mad just thinking about it!" Atim spoke through gritted teeth.

"Well, you shouldn't get more upset about it than Chickadee, it didn't happen to you." Sam shook his head at his brother.

Atim was about to retort when Otter spoke.

"Chickadee wasn't the only one who had a bad day yesterday." Otter gave the biggest Muskrat a little nudge. Atim looked at the ceiling, then rubbed his eyes.

Sam told Chickadee about the mugging and their escape.

"Are you serious!?" Chickadee was the next one to cough and spit cereal across the table.

"If it hadn't been for the old, scraggly cab driver..." Sam shook his head.

"Cabbie John saved us!" Otter declared.

"Can't judge a book by its cover, that's for sure." Atim pursed his lips.

"So...is there any money left?" Chickadee asked the group.

Atim pulled out his pockets. Samuel shook his head. Otter shrugged.

"Brett and his buddies took it all," Atim admitted sadly as he swiped the hair away from his eyes.

Chickadee's heart fell when she heard it. "Brett?"

"Yeah, Brett." Samuel nodded slowly.

"But…" Chickadee was speechless. She couldn't figure how this was possible.

"He scammed us!" Atim threw up his hands. "His buddy punched Otter." He threw a hand out in his cousin's direction. "And Brett took them there."

"The big bully from the pool game said that was a scam too. I thought Brett hooking himself seemed kind of strange. I guess, for me, that's when the doubts started," Samuel recollected.

Chickadee's mind went over the past few days and all the little things that told her Brett had changed. He wasn't the Brett she liked in Windy Lake. She decided to put it behind her. Like the walk in the rain yesterday, she wasn't going to let it bother her today.

"So, what are we going to do then?" Chickadee raised an eyebrow at her cousins. The boys squinted hard but couldn't seem to squeeze out any new ideas.

"Okay," she said. "I propose we focus on Auntie Charlotte. I spent yesterday looking for Grandpa's sister. I've hit a dead-end, but I've got a lead on another place where we may be able to find info."

"It would be pretty cool to find Grandpa's sister after all this time. Why the dead-end?" Samuel was pinching his lower lip.

"We need her exact date of birth or else we can't go any farther." Chickadee slurped the last of the milk out of her cereal bowl. "I'm pretty sure the lady at the adoption registry knew more than she was saying, but she's using the date of birth as the key for unlocking the information."

"Is that what they call red tape?" Sam's brow furrowed.

"I don't know, but her assistant was helpful. She told me to go to the National Centre for Truth and Reconciliation, the N-C-T-R, she called it. That's where they keep a lot of the information on residential schools." Chickadee looked around at her cousins who nodded.

"I want to go down there and find out as much as we can. If we can find out more, it might unlock the archives info, and we may actually get somewhere." She stood and gathered all their dirty dishes and put them on the counter near the dishwasher.

After using the computer to find the NCTR's address, the Mighty Muskrats headed out. The bus dropped them off in the middle of a large university campus.

"Who knew the NCTR was in the same location where Harold is going to school?" Atim looked around at the maze of different buildings.

"We're the new ones figuring things out." Sam chuckled at his brother. "Probably everybody else knew it was here."

"Could be." Atim nodded sagely.

Samuel looked at the map they had printed off at Auntie Sadie's. "I think, if we head…that way," he pointed down a path that led behind a cluster of buildings, "we'll find the place we're looking for."

The Muskrats walked between the buildings. When they got past them, they saw a large brick house tucked quietly away at the back of the university. It had once been a home, but it had long been converted to offices. The building had obviously been on the university grounds for many, many years. Its three stories looked tiny beside the huge buildings full of classrooms, libraries, and labs. The comfortable bundle of bricks now stored all the research brought together by the Truth and Reconciliation Commission of Canada as it delved into the history of residential schools.

CHAPTER 15

A Centre for Truth and Reconciliation

The Mighty Muskrats entered quietly. The inside of the building was cozy, with softwood windowsills and banisters and hardwood floors. The walls were filled with a mixture of art and interesting research in the form of letters, official documents, and ancient photos squeezed in between a phalanx of bookshelves. Well-used desks, printers, and office tables held down the open spaces.

A thirty-something lady was working at a desk nearby. Her smile was bright as she spoke. "Hello. Can I help you?"

Chickadee stepped forward with her cousins in tow. "Hello, Ma'am. We're looking for information on our great-aunt Charlotte. We know she went to the Chokecherry Pass Residential School."

The woman stood and walked over to the Muskrats. It was obvious the Centre had once been an old house.

The lady's office was squeezed in what would have been the hallway and greeting area, the museum and research portions were spread over the former dining room and living room.

"My name is Meher." She shook each of their hands. "Have you been here before?"

"No. We're from up north. I'm Atim," Atim—obviously stricken by Meher's beauty—said with a goofy smile.

The other Muskrats rolled their eyes and then gave her their names in turn.

"Well, you came to the right place when it comes to looking for information on your great-aunt. We have a computer catalogue of information and enrollment lists of all the residential schools. Come with me."

As they followed Meher into the former dining room to a row of three computers, she gave them a spiel that she had no doubt delivered numerous times before.

"At the National Centre for Truth and Reconciliation, we maintain a lot of the records and files that have been collected from residential schools as well as a large library of documents written about those schools. For over a century and a half, residential schools operated in Canada. Over 150,000 children attended them. Often underfunded and overcrowded, the schools were used as a tool of assimilation by the Canadian state and churches. Thousands of students suffered abuse. All suffered from loneliness and a longing to be home with their families. The damages inflicted by residential schools continue to this day."

She took them to a long table with a few computers on it.

"You can access our database here." Meher leaned over, took the mouse, and began to click options on the screen.

"Where did you say she went?" Meher smiled at Chickadee.

"Chokecherry Pass, it's up north." Chickadee studied the home page of www.nctr.ca on a nearby computer screen. "What kind of work do you do here? I know you keep stuff…but what do you do?"

"Well, do you know there was the Truth and Reconciliation Commission, which studied residential schools and the experiences of the students?" Meher looked at each of the Muskrats. They all nodded. They had heard stories of the residential schools from their Elders, uncles, and aunties. They had been told about the apology and the Truth and Reconciliation Commission in school.

"Okay. That's good to hear." Meher smiled. "So…as the permanent home for all the statements, documents, and other materials gathered by the Commission, the Centre acts as a storehouse so those of us here can educate everyone in Canada about this terrible tragedy. But education means different things to different audiences. For many Canadians, who are at a beginner level when it comes to learning about residential schools, we produce materials and hold classes that tell people of this wrong committed against Indigenous families and nations. Of course, there are people with a higher level of knowledge, but they still want to learn more. We have those old files from the government, churches, and the schools themselves to study and research that level of detailed learning. And many First Nations people come here, like you, to learn more about their families."

"Seems like a pretty important subject for people to know about," Samuel said, crossing his arms and trying to sound grown up.

Meher nodded. "It's important for all Canadians to remember that it is wrong for any government to take children away from their families so that they can be forcefully assimilated. If we don't remember our history, there is always the chance we will repeat it. Now, let's find the Chokecherry Pass files."

Her fingers clicked against the keyboard. The computer thought for a moment and then spit out a list of documents, dates, and data.

"We have a lot of documents on Chokecherry Pass. What you want to look for is the enrollment lists, which will be catalogued by years. See this?" Meher pointed at the screen and made sure she had Chickadee's attention. "This is a scan of an enrollment list, but this example is the wrong year. See that number? Okay. You want to find one that matches the years your great-aunt went to Chokecherry. Think you can do that?"

Chickadee nodded enthusiastically. She had wanted to get in the driver's seat since she first saw the computer and heard the word *database*. Meher smiled, stepped back, and gestured for Chickadee to take over.

Chickadee pulled over a nearby office chair and sat down in front of the computer. She studied the list of information in front of her. Samuel also grabbed a chair and sat down beside her.

Meher watched them for a moment and then returned to her desk. Atim and Otter followed the young woman. In the area where she worked, dozens of wooden tiles, about half the size of a cracker, had been applied to the walls. Each one had a painted picture, design, or message. The wall was covered in tiny works of art by hundreds of different people. From faces to flowers to fishes to figures, a multitude of different ideas and feelings spoke from the collection of tiny tiles.

"These are cool!" Atim poked at one of the tiles and smiled at Meher.

"Please don't touch that," she chided. Atim pulled his paw back quickly. His face was a mixture of horror and embarrassment.

Otter snickered.

Meher's chuckle tinkled. "I mean, they're only glued on, we have kids picking them off all the time. You don't look like a kid."

Atim beamed, but then he quickly put on his serious

face. "I never thought of that. Of course, kids would pick them off. But they're wonderful expressions of color and… uh…art." He pushed on the tile he had been picking at to make sure it was stuck to the wall. "So…" he seemed desperate to keep the conversation going, "…what do you like most about your work?"

Meher turned her attention back to her computer. "The learning, I suppose. Listening to the teachings of the Elders is wonderful. Listening to the survivors can be hard. There are so many sad stories, but there are good stories too. My education is in research and history. I like… understanding the past and how people thought in the past."

"I could listen to Elders all day…sometimes." Atim moved, so he had a better view of Meher's face as she worked. He leaned against a doorframe. Otter picked up a pamphlet and started reading.

"See this?" Meher pointed to a logo on a poster pasted above her desk. Atim took the opportunity to move closer. He leaned over her desk and studied the logo closely. The symbol was a circle, split into four crescents, that surrounded two intertwined flames. Atim blinked, like an optical illusion the logo seemed to change, the two flames were now stylized birds in flight.

"The seven tongues of flame represent the Seven Sacred Teachings. We try to include Indigenous perspectives and values in all that we do. It's not just what you do, it's how you do it, so we try to include Indigenous ways of doing things in how we do things too." Meher continued to look at her screen as she spoke.

"Like the smudging?" Otter waved at the air and sniffed. The smell of smoldering sweetgrass hung lightly in the air.

"Like the smudging, but it's much more than that. Indigenous people had ways of collecting, storing, and transmitting information. There are strong traditions of storytelling, organizing their people, and healing. We try to incorporate these ideas in our work." Meher smiled proudly.

"A lot of healing…." Otter winced a little as he thought back to the stories he'd been told about the older generations of his family.

"Yes, we had a residential school Survivor here the other day. She told us about how, as a child, she once went to help a girl in the schoolyard. The girl was fresh from her community and had been injured playing. In her pain, the new girl spoke Cree. The lady who visited us wanted to help the new girl and spoke Cree back to her. Seems natural, right?"

Atim and Otter nodded.

Meher shook her head. "Well, they both got the strap for speaking their language."

The boys looked at her, wide-eyed.

"That's terrible…." Atim scowled and shook his head.

"That was just the assimilation part of it. As I said, it's not only what you do, it's how you do it. The government took the kids away, but then they didn't fund the schools well or push for good education standards. They didn't make sure the kids were safe in their care either. They made a bad system even worse by how they carried it out."

Meher looked at Otter sadly. "A lot of times, uncaring people were hired. They looked down at the kids and their parents. Sometimes bad people who hurt the kids were hired. And these were *residential* schools, which means the students lived there. Every school has its bullies, but imagine if you *lived* with the bullies in your school 24-7, and some of them were your teachers! Proper supervision for all the children was needed, but that wasn't carried out either."

"What a mess!" Atim smacked his forehead and wiped his hand down his face.

"It was a mess, and it is a difficult topic. We also have many residential school Survivors tell us about good things that happened at the schools. There were many people who worked at the schools who really cared about the students. Many of the schools had hockey teams and other activities that the students may not have been able to access back home."

"But it was the *purpose* of the schools that was really wrong, wasn't it?" Otter frowned at Meher.

"Yes, any good that may have happened could never

overcome the intent of the system. Nor could the people working at the schools overcome the wrong way the system was carried out—the underfunding and lack of supervision in 'taking care of' thousands of children and teenagers, in many different landscapes, across the second-largest country in the world."

Atim and Otter were lost in their own thoughts about all that they had just heard.

Meher smiled and stood up. "Let's check on what the others have found, shall we?" She led them back to their cousins.

CHAPTER 16

A Face from the Past

Chickadee and Samuel were intently and happily look-ing through documents on the database. Chickadee had hoped to be able to save the research they found to show Grandpa. She plugged the memory stick she brought with her into the computer tower. A collage of tabs was splat-tered across the screen.

"Find anything interesting?" Meher smiled at the in-tensity of the Muskrats' study.

"Oh, yes!" Chickadee tapped the corner of the screen and beamed at Meher. "There is so much stuff here!"

Samuel straightened the screen and took over con-trol of the mouse. "We wanted to ask you about some stuff." He brought up a scan of a yellowed paper. "What is this?"

Meher studied the contents of the document. "Oh, okay. This was during the implementation of the Indian

Agent system. Agents were appointed by the government to enforce their rules and control First Nations. So, what happened here was, a First Nations farmer had some hay to sell. The principal of Chokecherry wanted to buy the hay, but this letter is the principal telling the First Nations farmer that he had to get permission from his Indian Agent first."

"He had to get permission to sell his own hay?" Atim's lip curled.

"Correct," Meher said. "That was the law for First Nations under the Indian Agent system, from about 1876 to 1976. You didn't want to get the agent angry because he controlled your community and its resources."

"We figured it was something like that. We couldn't believe it!" Samuel shook his head. "What about this one?" He brought up another tab with an old letter.

Meher bent to look at the screen again. "All right, this is…this is, well, basically, a threat letter." Meher kept reading.

"I knew it!" Samuel smacked his hand on his cheek in disbelief.

"What?!" Atim moved beside Meher to read the screen. Once he was there, he couldn't read, he just thought about how close he was to the attractive woman.

"It's a letter that was given to us by a parent of children within Chokecherry Pass. They got it from their Indian Agent. It's basically saying, if the parent left the First

Nations lands to go hunting that fall, their children would not be allowed to come home from residential school for Christmas."

Atim stopped pretending to read the screen and stood up straight.

Meher straightened too and looked around at all the Muskrats. "This actually touches on what I'm doing my book on for my doctorate; how the children in residential schools were used against their parents back on the First Nations."

"Like when they refer to real people as pawns in a game of chess?" Samuel pinched his lower lip.

"Exactly," Meher said. "The Canadian government was trying to take control of First Nations without having to spend a lot of resources. Access to their children was often used as both a carrot and a stick against their families. The government in Ottawa, and the local Indian Agents in each area, used the children in residential schools when they wanted to control the parents. Would you listen to someone, if they had your kids far away in a government building?"

"You'd have to." Samuel lifted his palms skyward, and the other Muskrats nodded.

Meher put her hands on her hips and addressed Chickadee. "What else have you found?"

"Well, we found scans of student lists that have Auntie Charlotte's name, but some of them have three girls with the same name. Some of them have dates of birth, but which one is hers?"

"Hmm. Your Auntie's name wasn't uncommon at the time." Meher looked closer at the screen. Chickadee clicked through the other lists at Meher's request.

"Yes," Meher said thoughtfully. "You're going to have to keep looking for something that will give you another clue. This is the way research is sometimes. You use the who, what, where, when, and why of what you're looking for to find a direction. But then you need to go deeper into the details to get clarification of that one bit of information you need."

The researcher left the Muskrats to keep digging into the mountain of information on the screen. They all gathered around Chickadee.

"So…now what?" Chickadee looked around her at her cousins.

"What would Grandpa say?" Samuel asked, searching through the list on the screen.

"Know what you're hunting. Know the land you're hunting on." Otter smiled as he said it in his Grandpa's gruff voice. Atim laughed and slapped him on the back.

"Okay." Sam said. "The landscape is the database. It's full of written documents and pictures. We're looking for Auntie Charlotte. We want her date of birth, but…" There was a long pause as he stared off into space.

"You know, she's not just numbers. She has a face too,

right?" Chickadee suddenly turned her attention back to the search engine and began to refine her search.

"Of course!" Sam followed Chickadee's actions on the screen. Atim and Otter gathered around the computer and quietly watched. Chickadee searched the Chokecherry Pass files for class pictures. A bunch came up.

"Too much!" Chickadee's fingers attacked the keyboard again, narrowing the query to the years and grades when Auntie Charlotte was in the school. A handful of links were offered.

"That's better." She clicked on the first link, and a black-and-white class picture from long ago sprang up on the screen. About thirty children stood on some steps leading up to a large door. They were all dressed in the same bland clothing and were flanked by two nuns and a priest. It seemed nobody had said "Say cheese!" before the picture was taken. The Muskrats looked deeply into the photo, studying the faces.

"Enlarge it." Samuel flicked Chickadee on the shoulder. She clicked the mouse a few times and the students' heads grew from raisins to plums. It was much easier to make out their features now, but it was still difficult in the grainy, black-and-white photo.

After they had a look, and agreed there was no one that resembled family, they moved on to the next picture. It was the same scene, different children. They all leaned in and began studying the faces of students from long ago.

"There!" Otter pointed to a girl standing in the second row. She looked like a young Grandpa with long hair. The Muskrats were silent as they all studied the girl.

Chickadee suddenly remembered her dream from a few nights before. This was the girl she had connected to in her dream. This was the girl who had stepped out of the fog.

"She is standing so straight, so serious," Atim whispered.

"Just like Grandpa in his pictures," Otter suggested. "It looks like she's saying, 'I want to go home.'"

"They all are." Chickadee pointed to a few of the faces.

"Auntie Charlotte would have already been at the school for over a year on the date this photo was taken. At eight or nine, she was away from her mom and her family." Chickadee stared at the image. She imagined what it was like to be that girl, standing on those steps, being taken care of by strangers, having your brothers and sisters so close but being forbidden to speak with them, and not knowing if you'd ever see your mom again.

"Look here, this photo is one of two." Samuel pointed to the screen. "Try the next in the set, maybe it will have a list of students. We have to confirm that it's her."

Chickadee hated to leave the face on the screen, but she clicked on the link to the next picture. It was a scan of the back of the class photo. Someone had handwritten the children's names on the reverse in a messy script.

"Look at that." Chickadee pointed to a "W" and "L"trapped in brackets beside Auntie Charlotte's name.

"Windy Lake." Atim stood and smiled.

"We found her," Chickadee whispered. She looked up at her cousins. The boys gathered around her, and the Mighty Muskrats shared a hug.

"Well, now we know what she looked like." Samuel slapped Atim on the back.

"Grandpa will want to see his little sister. Can we get a copy?" Otter stared at the little girl that was from his family so long ago.

"That would be so cool. We'll ask if we can get a hard copy." Chickadee hugged Otter again and then sat back down at the computer. "I want to go back and see the en-rollment scans again. Now that we have a year and a class, it may help me find a list with her info on it."

"Good idea," Samuel said as he also reclaimed his seat. Atim and Otter chuckled at their highly-focused peers, they put an arm over each other's shoulders and leaned in to see what new clues might be found.

Back at the search engine, Chickadee focused her que-ry once again using the information from the photo about Auntie Charlotte's year and class. In a few moments, she found one of the student lists with more information on their great-aunt. Under the column "D.O.B.", there was no month or day, but "Spring 1951" was listed beside Auntie Charlotte's name.

The male Muskrats high fived each other. Chickadee allowed herself a tight smile as she celebrated the find. At the same time, she wondered if it would be enough.

The celebration caught the attention of Meher who came to see what it was all about. "Did you find what you were looking for?" She moved closer to look at the screen.

"We found Auntie Charlotte's face! Picture, I mean." Atim pointed at the computer.

"That's great! How about her date of birth?" Meher look at Chickadee.

"We found the years she was in Chokecherry *and* the year of her birth," Chickadee said proudly.

"That's a wonderful start." Meher nodded her approval. "Let me see."

She took control of the mouse and with the new information refined the search again. She clicked on a link and another scanned letter popped up. After reading a moment, she stepped back. "Look at this, it's a letter to the principal along with his response."

Chickadee and Samuel leaned in.

"It says," Meher continued, "that there was a request for a 'pleasant, hard-working young girl who could cook, clean, and do yard chores to be adopted. Your auntie Charlotte was suggested. It seems…she was sent to a difference province. But there's nothing else on her after that. Once she was adopted, she was out of the residential school system." Meher's wavy, dark hair bounced as she shook her head.

"A different province?" Samuel pinched his lower lip. "She could be thousands of miles away!"

Chickadee's shoulders slumped.

"Hey, you got us two new clues, Chickadee. Now we know what she looked like." Atim shook her shoulder roughly until she reluctantly smiled.

"She's a real person to us now," Otter told his cousin. "I can't wait to find her."

"Now, we can go back to the adoption registry and, hopefully, unlock that info!" Samuel looked off into the distance, already planning next steps.

Meher allowed them to put what they found on the memory stick. They printed out Auntie Charlotte's class photo.

"What's wrong?" Meher asked Chickadee after seeing the frown on her face. The boys gathered around and waited for their cousin's answer.

"I don't know. After seeing her face…she looks like my grandpa." Chickadee looked at the ground and then back at Meher. "She seemed so sad in that school. And Grandpa said he wasn't allowed to speak his language while in residential school. Now, none of my cousins speak Cree…." Chickadee trailed to a stop.

"Yes?" Meher reached out and squeezed her arm.

"My grandpa says, there are many roads to walk after

we go on our final journey from this world. Sometimes, we have old Cree souls, like reincarnation. Sometimes, we're our ancestors." The boys nodded. They had heard the same lesson.

"Yes. I have heard some Elders express this before." Meher's face was serious.

"Well…what happens if your soul speaks Cree, but your body speaks English?"

Meher looked at Chickadee, impressed. "I don't know, but it would explain much of the need for healing that many residential school Survivors feel. My people, from India, are also working through their own healing process due to colonialism. But the difference is, we always outnumbered the colonists. This is why we were able to take back our lands."

"I think bringing back the language is an important part of that healing. In our family, the older generations speak Cree, but no one in our generation does. We can't let the residential school system win," Sam said, in agreement with his cousin.

"We need to speak the language of our souls," Otter added quietly. Atim nodded.

As the Muskrats were getting ready to leave, Meher took Chickadee aside. "You have great computer skills. You'd make an excellent researcher, Chickadee."

Chickadee blushed.

Meher gave her a friendly hug. "You're not very used to getting compliments, are you?"

Chickadee stared at the floor and shrugged.

"That's okay. You'll get used to it. Keep doing what you are doing. Ask questions, find answers, push for details. I'd like to see you here at the university one day."

Chickadee was grateful and slightly embarrassed at the same time. Quietly, she thanked Meher for her words and her help.

After quick good-byes from the boys, the Mighty Muskrats were soon waiting at the bus stop to head back to Auntie Sadie's.

CHAPTER 17

Red Tape Tangle

"Well, that's that. We can go wander around the mall today!" Atim said, as they sat on the fold-out bed in Auntie Sadie's basement.

"No." Chickadee frowned. "We have new info we can use. Besides, Harold said we aren't allowed to go to the mall anymore. We can go to the post-adoption registry and see if we can find out more about Auntie Charlotte."

"I don't know." Atim fell back on the bed and held his head. "Can't we take a day off?"

"The trail is still fresh, right?" Chickadee looked at Otter.

Slowly, Otter nodded.

"Look, Grandpa gave us this mission. Grandpa!" Chickadee searched the faces of her cousins. "I don't know, but if we could find his little sister…maybe it would pay him back for all he has given us, right?"

Finally, Sam and Otter nodded enthusiastically.

"Oooohhh, all right!" Atim groaned. "We'll go to the post-adoption registry."

The other Muskrats jumped off the bed and started getting ready to go. Atim slowly followed.

☆

"You again!" the security guard at the registry building said with mock indignation as he recognized Chickadee from earlier in the week. "Who are your friends?" The old man stood, walked over to the elevators, and pressed the button for them.

"My cousins," Chickadee said. "You were so kind the first time, I had to come back."

"Well, we're happy to have you. Second floor, again?" The guard stood with his fists on his hips and grinned down at them. "We don't get too many kids coming to the post-adoption registry."

"We're looking for our auntie. She was taken in the Sixties Scoop." Samuel also waited for the elevator with his fists on his hips.

"Well, I hope you find her." He looked at Chickadee. "You made it home okay the other day?"

Chickadee squinted and put her head to one side. She stuck out her hand and waggled it back and forth.

"The city takes some time to get used to. I was a farm

boy long ago." He chuckled. "When I first moved here, I remember I could never sleep in the city because of all of the noise. Then, one day, I went back to the farm for a visit. And I couldn't fall asleep because of the quiet!"

Ding! The elevator doors opened. Atim and Otter stepped in.

"Bye!" Chickadee and Sam said as they joined their cousins.

"What goes up, must come down." The guard waved as the doors closed.

"Was that weird?" Samuel raised his eyebrow at the others.

Otter held up two fingers close together and whispered, "L'il bit."

"It was uplifting." Atim guffawed. He poked Chickadee with his elbow. "Get it? Because we're in an elevator."

"Yeah, I got it." She elbowed Atim back.

The elevator doors opened. They walked in a huddle to the counter and Samuel rang the bell.

Janice popped her head around the wall and then stepped into the public service area when she saw Chickadee.

"Hello, Chickadee. Are these your brothers?" Janice smiled at the boys.

The Muskrats giggled.

"Cousins." Chickadee grinned. "But they're like brothers. Most of my boy cousins are."

"That must be nice." Janice leaned on to the counter. "How can I help you?"

"We found Auntie Charlotte's year of birth." Chickadee's voice was cautious, knowing it wasn't a full date of birth. "We were told she was born in the spring of 1951."

"Well…Mrs. Yenna is here. I have to speak to her about it. Give me a sec." Janice disappeared.

Mrs. Yenna appeared and studied each of the children in turn.

"Have you found your family-member's date of birth?" she asked when she recognized Chickadee.

"Well, we have the season and the year." Chickadee looked hopeful as she handed the lady hard copies of the documents they had found. The woman took the papers and read them. She typed the information into the computer.

Chickadee hated being on the hind end of a computer screen. However, reflected in the lady's eyeglasses, Chickadee could sort of see the computer screen. She could tell it blinked blank as the computer searched for the data that was put into its system, and then, after a few moments, a long stream of information scrolled out. The lady read, her eyes skipping back and forth across the document. The Muskrats waited quietly.

Finally, Mrs. Yenna huffed. She looked at Chickadee.

"I'm sorry, we still do not have enough information to distinguish your relative from others."

"What?" Chickadee's voice held a touch of anger. She took a deep breath.

Samuel stepped forward. "My cousin Chickadee has done an amazing job of finding the information that we have so far, and in a short period of time. What's stopping you from giving us what you have?"

"There are strong rules around privacy. We need a full date of birth. There are two people in your community who have the same name. We need a full birth date to make sure we're telling you about the right person."

"Was the other person born in the same year?" Chickadee probed.

"I can't tell you that." Mrs. Yenna shook her head and slipped out of the chair. "Please, come back when you have all the information required."

Chickadee's shoulders fell.

"Ma'am, is there any way you can help us?" Atim pleaded.

"I am bound by the rules that govern the registry," Mrs. Yenna said, as she walked away.

The Muskrats gathered around each other.

"What do we do now?" Chickadee's face was full of sorrow. "I wanted to find her for Grandpa. Now, we're stuck...and that lady knows more than she is saying!"

"She does." Otter looked over his shoulder to make sure that Mrs. Yenna wasn't standing there. Janice watched the Muskrats with a face full of inner conflict.

"It'll be okay, cuz. Grandpa will understand." Atim gave Chickadee a one-armed hug.

Samuel was staring off into the distance as he tried to think of next steps.

They heard a loud sigh. "I can't...." Janice shook her head. She closed her eyes and covered half her face with a hand. She opened her eyes and it was obvious a decision had been made.

She looked at her watch. "Today I'm eating lunch at the Sub Station down the block at noon. You'll find it if you turn left out the front doors. Okay?" She looked at the Muskrats seriously.

The Muskrats nodded in unison.

"Have a good day." She turned on her heel and disappeared from the client services area.

The Muskrats hustled out of the little room. They all shared the feeling of wanting to get some place where they could talk openly. The door to the stairwell was close by. Atim opened it.

"Ho-leh!" Atim smacked his leg as they walked down the stairs. "She was trying to tell us something, right?"

Samuel laughed at his brother. "You're quick, Sherlock."

"Her heart was hurting," Otter said, sincerely.

"She was nice, right from the beginning." Chickadee's brow furrowed. "But she's scared of her boss, right?"

The boys nodded.

"So, what do you want to do?" Sam asked his cousins, already knowing the answer.

The other Muskrats laughed at the question. There was no other choice than the Sub Station.

CHAPTER 18

An Ally Takes a Risk

The Muskrats waited on the concrete steps of the big office building that held the sandwich shop. Eventually, they saw Janice walking toward them. She waved excitedly once she spotted them.

After quick hellos, Janice pulled a piece of paper from her purse.

"I couldn't stand by and watch that happen," Janice said apologetically to the Muskrats. "The information is there, and you have a right to see it. I don't know, sometimes I feel like we make this harder than it needs to be."

"Did you quit your job...?" Chickadee stepped toward Janice, worried.

"Well, no." Janice looked at the ground. "I have bills to pay, I can't do that, but I *can* give you this." She held out the piece of paper.

Chickadee took it and began to read.

"Mrs. Yenna is a by-the-book kind of person." Janice shrugged as she spoke to Samuel. "That's probably why she's good at a place like the adoption archives. She'd fire me if she knew I gave you that."

"Knowledge is power." Sam's brow furrowed. "They've got it all locked up."

"Yes, and that's what I can't be a part of. If we really want to create reconciliation with First Nations people, we have to realize that the power is one-sided. And the only way there will be healing is to give some of it back," Janice said.

"This paper says Auntie Charlotte was sent to Alberta for adoption. She was in the care of an old lady. But then the woman passed away. She was in her late eighties, so probably just old age. But then, that's it." Chickadee continued to study the paper.

"I read it myself," Janice said through tight lips. "She was there, but then she was gone. I looked for more information under that name, but if there is other data, it isn't in this province."

Chickadee was disappointed they had hit a dead-end. But Janice's help made this disappointment easier somehow.

"It's funny, Mrs. Yenna wouldn't tell you anything, but that didn't stop her from talking to me about it. She says it wasn't uncommon for adopted kids to be passed down to a close relative of the adoptive family. She said, sometimes, the children were even renamed."

"So, that's it?" Chickadee frowned.

"Yes, I guess. The trail ends when she left the system." Janice gave a half smile and a one-shoulder shrug.

"Even if she is still alive, she's probably thousands of miles away!" Chickadee squeaked.

The young lady from the registrar nodded sadly.

"Grandpa will be happy to know she grew to be an adult," Samuel said.

"We don't really know if she did," Janice cautioned.

"Is it likely?" Samuel raised an eyebrow at her.

Janice thought for a moment and then nodded slowly. "I hope you find her. I hope...you know, the Canada I want is one where we don't have First Nations families looking for lost loved ones. As a Canadian, I believe that our country will be better off when your communities are better off. I just...want to do my part, you know?"

Otter was closest to her, so he gave Janice a hug.

"Thank you!" Sam said to her. "I guess we might as well get along, right?"

"Listen, I brought this too." Janice brought out a handful of papers married with a staple. Samuel reached out, so she handed it to him. "These papers, your grandpa can fill them out. That would let the registry know that if your great-aunt wants to reach out to him, he would be open to meeting her."

Samuel's eyes went wide. "You mean, if she has a similar request in right now, we could find out her information?"

"Yes!" Janice smiled.

Chickadee clapped her hands. A smile spread from ear to ear.

"I have to go." The young woman turned to Chickadee and touched her arm. "I hope this gives your grandfather… something."

"It will!" Chickadee assured her with a smile. She hugged Janice and watched her walk away.

CHAPTER 19
Muskrat Maelstrom

"Unless we're going to go to Alberta, we're at the end of the trail." Atim's hand made a cutting motion through the air.

Back at Auntie Sadie's, the Muskrats had a case meeting in the basement. Samuel studied the papers while his brother sat on the edge of the mattress and played an old video game on an ancient TV. Otter and Chickadee leaned against the back of the couch and watched Atim play.

Chickadee shrugged. "Janice gave us some hope. She gave us these papers. Maybe Auntie Charlotte is looking for us too."

"Looks like Grandpa would have to sign them. He'd be her 'if possible, closest biological relative,' right?" Samuel pointed to a line on the paper.

The sound of Auntie Sadie's voice snapped them out of their thoughts.

"We're home!"

Immediately, their younger cousins' footsteps could be heard coming down the stairs in a tumble. Nitanis took a running leap onto the bed. David moseyed into the room behind her.

"My mom is going to take you guys to the Exhibition Fair tomorrow!" Nitanis's eyes were bright with excitement.

"We're still going to day care," David moped.

Auntie Sadie appeared in the doorway of the rec room, her hands weighed down with grocery bags, she smiled at her niece and nephews.

"Hey guys. So, you can go to the Ex tomorrow. Harold has the morning off. I was going to get him to take you, but I can drop you off and pick you up later. Cool?" A ripple went through her eyebrows when she didn't get the expected reaction.

The Muskrats looked at each other. Their aunt still didn't know their money had been taken by Brett and the bullies.

Chickadee glared at the boys.

The boys looked at each other guiltily but didn't say anything.

"Thanks, Auntie," Samuel said. "I think we need some time to talk about it."

"All right." Auntie Sadie sounded confused. "You guys okay?"

"Doing great, Auntie!" Atim took his hand off the

controller long enough to give her a thumbs up.

"Love you, Auntie." Chickadee waved.

"Ookaaay." Auntie Sadie's eyes narrowed as she stepped behind the wall and jogged back up the stairs to get dinner started. David and Nitanis ran after their mother.

"We need to tell her!" Chickadee whispered angrily.

"We could just go and hang around outside the fair. And then be there when she comes to pick us up." Atim nervously shook his head.

"Do you think Harold would go for that?" Samuel raised an eyebrow.

"Doubt it!" Otter snickered.

"Well, she's not going to be happy if we tell her we lost all our money!" Atim hissed.

"She'd never let us go out with you watching us again, that's for sure." Samuel shook his head at his brother.

"I guess, we haven't been, you know, too smart," Otter said with a sigh. "Wovoka's Wail is playing tonight."

"Ahh, poop!" Atim covered his face with his hands and then slouched forward. When he stopped rubbing his eyes, he looked at his cousin. "Sorry, Otter."

"Yeah, sorry, Otter. We tried. It would have been cool if you had been able to go see the Wail on your first visit to the city." Samuel lightly punched Otter on the shoulder.

"Otter!" Chickadee was annoyed. "I'm sorry too, but we got off track. We trusted Brett. We lost our money, and all for those stupid tickets."

"Chickadee...!" Otter reached out to her, his voice sad, but she pulled away.

"Well, you guys better figure something out because I ain't lying to Auntie." Chickadee quickly climbed off the fold-out.

Her cousins called her back, but Chickadee kept walking. She didn't look back as she went upstairs to the living room, slumped onto the couch, and snatched up the TV remote. She pressed the on button hard and angrily flipped from channel to channel.

CHAPTER 20

Connection

The backseat of the black car was big and noisy. She couldn't see over the front seat. Treetops and telephone lines were all she could see out the windows. She was afraid. She shouldn't be here. She didn't know these people. When the door opened, it wasn't in front of her home. An immense brick building blocked out the sun. She was given to a woman dressed in black and white. They took her clothes. They cut her hair. Long dark strands on the floor mixed with her tears. How could they do that without asking her mom? Her heart was sore. They scrubbed her then. Hard brushes rasped her skin until it was red. Thankfully, they gave her clothes. They weren't her clothes, but they were warm after the cold. She was in the darkness. To either side were white-washed beds, each holding a girl who was lonely, scared, and blinking back tears. She wanted her older brother. He would hold her. But he was curled up in a similar bed, in a similar room, on the other side of the school.

Time blurred. In class, she would watch the songbirds sitting on the bushes outside the window. In winter, little feet clasped twigs that bounced and danced in the wind. Black-and-white puffs of life, flittering feathers, seeking morsels in the frigid cold. And then she was one of them, looking back through the glass at a sad little girl, watching a chickadee outside the window. And the cold wind blew, and she held onto the little stick with all her might. But the wind was too strong, and it took her away. She fought and fought against the wind, but it pushed her toward the sunset. The wind took the breath from her lungs. She gasped for air. She tumbled as the landscape rushed below her. The prairies turned to foothills. A road struck straight across the yellows and greens of the treeless, rolling plains. A black spec crawled along that scar. The buffeting gale tossed her toward that dot, until it became a black car. And, suddenly, she was inside. A little girl pushing against the window. The popcorn crackle of the gravel road loud in her ears. They had traveled for so long. Her people were so far away. She could feel the distance in her heart. Could she still be herself without them? She wanted to be held by someone who would hug her back. She was so far away. She knew the black door would open… but what would be on the other side? The big black car crunched to a stop.

★

Chickadee woke with a start. Her surroundings alarmed her, unfamiliar shapes in the darkness. Where was she? Her heart was beating fast. And then she heard the familiar sound of Atim's snores in Auntie Sadie's basement. The dream had been so real, the feelings so raw. Her cheek was wet. Salty tears on the corner of her mouth. She would have to tell her Grandpa. Chickadee plopped back down on her pillow and went back to sleep.

CHAPTER 21

An Aunties' Anger

"I can't believe you lost your money and didn't tell me!" Auntie Sadie exploded. She was in the kitchen making her lunch before she left for work. Her eyes blazed with fury.

The Muskrats hung their heads. They had stopped eating their cereal and listened dejectedly.

When they had woken that morning, the boys agreed they must tell their aunt what had happened. It was a scary decision, but they all knew they couldn't lie to one of their Elders for long. Now, she blasted them as they sat at the table. David, Harold, and Nitanis were happy to be witnesses to their mother's anger and not the object of it. They smiled at their cousins over their bowls of cereal.

"The Crystal Place? Harold, what's that place like?"

"A palace!" Nitanis squealed, excitedly, before realizing she had misread the room. David snorted.

"It's just an arcade and pool hall, Mom." Harold shrugged as he slurped his milk. "Kinda in a sketchy neighborhood, but kids go there to play video games all the time."

Auntie Sadie turned to Atim. "I trust you to take care of your cousins, and this is what you do?"

Atim stared into his third bowl of Captain Crackles and didn't look up.

"They wouldn't have done it if it hadn't been for Musky's little brother. What's his name?" Harold played the lawyer for his younger cousins. The Muskrats dared not say a word.

"What's his name?" he prompted Chickadee.

"Brett!" she said, a little too loudly.

"Yeah, Brett. He's the one who took them there. He scammed them. And when they didn't get all the cash, him and his buddies jumped Otter and Sam." Harold twisted his face with derision at the bullies.

"Really?" His mother's brow furrowed. Harold nodded as he rose from the table and gathered his dirty bowl and spoon. "Really?" Auntie Sadie looked at the Muskrats.

They nodded as one. Nitanis giggled.

"There are always going to be people who will hurt you—who care about themselves more than they care about you!" she scolded. "That's no excuse for being stupid."

Auntie Sadie sighed. "When your uncle's away,

I'm here alone. I have to trust you guys to take care of yourselves."

"I'm sorry, Auntie." Samuel gave her a slight bow.

"It was my fault. I wanted Otter to go to the Wail concert so badly." Atim was unable to look his auntie in the eye.

"We all lost our money in the pool hall." Chickadee had long ago decided to take her punishment for the decision. Otter nodded in agreement with his cousin.

"Well, without your money, there's no point in taking you to the Exhibition. I don't have any extra cash." Auntie Sadie threw up her hands. "I guess that means you got the morning off, Harold."

Harold looked at his dejected little cousins. They were all studying the floor.

"You know...before I had to take you brats to the Exhibition, I was going to go to the Spence Street Fair. I volunteer for the Indigenous Art and Music Board, and we're putting on a street fest today."

"A street fest?" Samuel's guilty frown faded.

"This city has neighborhood street fests. Well, the better off neighborhoods anyway. The Board, we call it the I-AM Board, helps put on street fests in some of the poorer neighborhoods. We set up a stage, invite Indigenous musicians to come, and we light up a barbeque. We fed over three hundred people hot dogs, chips, and juice at Spence Street last year."

"I'm not sure they deserve to go to that even." Auntie Sadie's face was serious. Like all their aunties, her anger was hot and fearful, but it cooled quickly when she saw real remorse. There was still the matter of punishment though. "In my day, Grandma would tell you to go cut yourself a switch."

The Muskrats looked at each other, wide-eyed.

"I could make them volunteer at the street fest. Make them work." Harold offered, a slight smile on his face.

"Well, as long as you actually make them work. I don't want them just listening to music all day." Auntie Sadie stood with her hands on her wide hips, her voice held a touch of warning.

"There's always stuff to do. Especially, if we get there early. We always need help with set up."

Auntie Sadie thought a bit. "I took a bit of the morning off to take these boneheads to the fair, but then I have to go to work, and these kids have day care. I suppose I can drop you all off on my way to the hospital."

The Muskrats nodded enthusiastically.

CHAPTER 22

Lolly Pops

"Thanks for volunteering. Around here, we go by the philosophy; if you want something to happen, you got to make it happen!"

The chair of the I-AM Board lifted a heavy bag of charcoal out of the back of a truck and brought it over to the barbeque. Alan was a well-muscled, good-looking Anishinaabe man with glasses and a wide smile. He dropped the bag and then clapped his hands to get the dust off. He indicated the park with a wave. "There's plenty of stuff to do, if you see someone working, ask them if they need help and then get to it."

"Can I help you with these bags?" Atim flexed his muscles. After getting a nod, he ran back to the truck and rolled a big bag onto his shoulder.

Harold laughed and spoke to Chickadee. "That's Alan. Isn't he gorgeous? He's a good organizer too."

"Everyone here is a volunteer?" Samuel shielded his eyes with one hand as he looked around. Harold nodded.

They were in the clearing of a well-treed park. The barbeque and the food tent were set up along the east edge. A stage was being unfolded at the south end of the field. It was built on a medium-sized trailer that could be pulled behind a regular truck. With walls that folded out and down, it easily turned into a platform that could comfortably hold a five-piece band with drums, lights, and speakers.

"He looks like he needs help." Otter pointed to a young man wrestling with a long, colorful band of plastic in the wind. The banner would not unfurl. It lifted high in the wind and then wrapped itself around the head and body of the volunteer like a red, white, and blue tentacle. The young man struggled to detangle as the end of the banner flapped happily in the breeze.

"Let's go save that guy from the wind." Harold chuckled.

Over the next hour, the Muskrats helped set up the area for the crowd. When the first musicians arrived, the boys happily helped them move and arrange equipment. Chickadee kept close to her cousin Harold as he flitted from friend to friend, helping out in his own creative way.

Eventually, the music started, and the people of Spence Street began to show up. It was a poor neighbor-hood, full of new immigrants from Asia, Africa, Europe, and the north. Elders of all colors, children of all sizes, and adults of all creeds clapped and listened in the summer sunshine. Just before lunch, the barbeque was fired up and people lined up for food. The Muskrats helped the other volunteers make sure that everyone got a juice box, a bag of chips, and a hot dog.

Alan watched over everything to make sure it went off well. By mid-afternoon the charcoal was starting to run out, so he sent Harold and the boys out to get some more. When they returned, Harold and the male Muskrats unloaded the big bags. Job finished, they all went to see Chickadee, who was aproned and working behind a fold-out table beside the barbeque. She was taking wieners from the chef, marrying them with buns, and then planting them on paper plates.

As the boys stood there, Chickadee began to giggle. "You don't see?" she whispered. The male Muskrats looked around. A band on the stage was playing classic rock. A crowd of about three hundred people sat or stood and listened to the music. Children ran in-and-out of the chatty pockets of slower moving adults. The boys could tell something was funny but didn't know what it was. The chef handed Chickadee another wiener. She giggled harder.

"What?! What are you laughing about?" Samuel hated not knowing secrets.

The chef handed Chickadee yet another wiener. "Here

you go, Chick-a-dee-dee-dee-dee!" He emphasized the syllables and extended her name like a real chickadee in the bush.

The boys finally looked at him. He was dark brown, tall, and thin, with long, black hair on one side of his head and a large shaved patch on the other. His goatee was thin and wispy. He wore a leather vest, jeans, cowboy boots, and an apron that said, "Bar-B-Who?"

Otter's mouth fell open. "You're...Lolly Leach!"

"Who?" Atim flicked the hair out of his eyes and squinted at the smiling rocker.

"It's him...the guitarist from Wovoka's Wail!" Otter was so intent on Lolly that he let his hot dog roll off his plate.

"It *is* him." Samuel's jaw dropped.

Chickadee laughed.

Lolly grabbed a paper plate and began to fill it with cooked wieners. "You guys heard of my band?"

"These are the cousins I told you about. That skinny one is the guitarist, Otter. He's the one we wanted to get into your show." Chickadee acted as though she'd known Lolly for years.

"Of course, we've heard of the Wail." Samuel excitedly squirted ketchup on his dog.

Atim already had a mouthful. "Vish yis doe date. Re-re, uhmeenit."

Lolly laughed. "Thanks. That means a lot."

Chickadee took off her apron and held it out to Otter. "Wanna try my job?"

Otter couldn't tell if he was the most afraid or the most excited he'd ever been in his life. He took the apron, then put buns on plates, and held them out to his idol. He was speechless and had to concentrate on keeping the plate steady.

"The secret to cooking a good hot dog is patience," Lolly said. The two worked in silence for a while.

"You know, First Nations fans are the best fans." Lolly nudged Otter on the shoulder.

"Really?" Otter's nervousness ebbed since he wasn't asked to speak. He preferred to listen.

"Yeppers. Other fans see me as a thing. I'm like a cool statue or mountain or landscape that they're taking a picture in front of, you know?"

Otter thought about it, and then nodded. "I guess, yeah."

"But Indigenous fans always just want to help. They don't know how they can help. But they want to push me forward, you know?"

Otter nodded and waited for more wieners to be ready.

"That's why I come to these things. I grew up poor, didn't have a lot, and wouldn't even have had that if it hadn't been for the people who volunteered to make our neighborhood better." Lolly opened another package of raw dogs and put them on the grill within reach of Otter's tongs.

"We need more people like that, I guess," Otter said, thoughtfully.

"Back in the old days, nobody got paid. It was your reputation and your ability to survive that had value when you were with others. If you want something to happen, you got to make it happen. Do what you can, right?" Lolly slapped Otter on the back.

Otter smiled and nodded.

"Doesn't matter if it's the city or the rez. Our beliefs work. We prepared our youth to go into the world. We have to do that again, but with the knowledge of city Elders. You got a vacuum cleaner, you automatically know you might need to get it fixed one day, right? How do you find what you need in the urban bush?" Lolly laughed at his play on words.

As the day wore on into the evening, the lineup for hot dogs was satisfied and the music got a little faster. Lolly got up and played a few songs with the last band of the street fest. The Muskrats stood at the front of the crowd and bathed in the music. With happy tears in their eyes, they had a group hug as the final ballad drew to a close.

CHAPTER 23

A Mile in City Moccasins

"All right, let's get this place cleaned up!" Alan got the volunteers moving as the last notes faded into the evening.

Tear-down began as soon as the crowd started to thin. The musicians unplugged and hauled their equipment away. The volunteers of the I-AM Board were packing up the banners and supplies to be used at the next street fest that would be held in a different inner-city neighborhood.

The sun was nearing the horizon as Chickadee and Otter carried boxes of plastic forks and knives across the parking lot to Alan's car. Brett skidded up on his bike. Otter dropped his box and stepped in front of Chickadee.

Brett saw the movement and winced.

"You guys don't trust me now. I guess I deserve that," Brett said sadly.

"Deserve what? Us thinking you're a jerk?" Chickadee spat angrily.

"Yeah, that," Brett said.

"We could have all been hurt. Otter *did* get hurt. You robbed us!" Chickadee shouted.

"I didn't touch anyone!" Brett said, defensively.

"You set us up." Otter's voice was quiet, but it quivered with anger. "We would never have met those guys if you hadn't taken us to that place."

"I can't believe we looked up to you once!" Chickadee waved her arm dismissively. "You've changed, Brett. Changed from when you were in Windy Lake."

"You guys have, like, no idea!" Brett had taken their anger for a while, but now shot back with some of his own. "You don't know what it's like not to know anyone. You don't know what it's like to be the new kid in the city, on a poor street."

"I would never scam you, Brett. Nobody could make me." Otter looked him in the eye as he said it.

"You don't know what it's like…." Brett shook his head. "Once they've got you…"

"Who's got you!?" Chickadee threw her hands in the air.

"Do you think those guys are my *friends*? Do you think I saw any of that money?" Brett shouted back. But then quieted down and looked off toward the rest of the volunteers working.

"Why doesn't your brother help you?" Chickadee put her hands on her hips.

"He's the one who got me into all this! My brother is a freakin' gangster! Those dudes at The Crystal Palace are, like, the junior team for my brother's crew."

"You didn't have to get us involved!" Otter flung his arm in an angry arc.

Brett looked at his feet and then off across the city. "Look, those guys are in my neighborhood, you know. There's no way, like, for my brother and I to get away from them." Brett's voice wavered. "You know, there's wolves in Windy Lake. But the inner city has a wolf pack in every neighborhood. And they're always there, watching."

"You're just making excuses, Brett," Chickadee said. She was angry at herself for once looking up to him.

"I didn't want to do what I did. I thought if we got the money during the game, that would be it. But he wanted it all." Brett spread his hands in surrender.

The cousins stared at him.

"So, they bully you too?" Otter watched carefully for Brett's response.

Brett's eyes were full of tears that wouldn't fall. He nodded slowly. "It's a gang. We basically have to pay to, like, work for them." Brett sighed, held his head with one hand. "My dad always said, every job is a soap opera. You know, like those shows on TV? There are always people who want to get farther up the ladder, people who bring their troubles to work, people who have emotional issues."

Chickadee and Otter nodded.

"Gangs are a soap opera that will get you killed. Beat up, at least. You always have to be, like, watching your back."

Chickadee and Otter looked at each other.

"I didn't mean for you to get hurt, Otter," Brett said.

"Well, I did...." Otter picked up his box and began walking to Alan's car once again.

Chickadee and Brett stared at each other a moment.

"We good?" Brett asked. His voice doubtful.

"How can I trust you?" Chickadee's voice was pleading. She hoped he would have an answer.

Brett shook his head and looked at the sky.

"I suppose I can forgive you for what happened to me." Chickadee's eyes were wet, then her voice took on an edge. "But I can't forgive what happened to the boys. I can't forgive what happened to Otter."

"I messed up," Brett said, his voice apologetic.

"Good-bye, Brett." Chickadee walked around him. The tears quietly rolled down her cheeks.

Brett said nothing for a moment, but then his voice was suddenly angry. "You wonder why I did what I did? This is why! Everyone goes back...goes back to Windy Lake. And I'm stuck here...with my brother. Nobody has our back! It's just us!"

Chickadee stopped and spoke over her shoulder. "I'm sorry you have to go through that. I really am. But they didn't know we existed. You didn't have to feed us to your wolf pack." Chickadee kept walking.

Brett pedaled away in the other direction.

CHAPTER 24

Hope from Home

"Lolly was so cool!"

Otter was over the moon with the memory of meeting his hero. He put the popcorn maker on the counter and plugged it into the kitchen wall. The Muskrats and Harold were looking for late-night snacks. They planned to spend the rest of the evening watching a movie. They were extremely grateful to Harold for the day they'd had.

"You're lucky. Meeting your hero can be a dangerous thing. They're not always like you expect them to be." Harold waved his hand in the air as though dismissing a bad memory.

"I never, ever thought I would meet him." Atim shook his head in wonder.

Harold shrugged. "I'm not too surprised. Apparently, Alan knows him, and Alan's been around for years. But really? The urban Indigenous community can be fairly small too." He chuckled.

"Is that why you volunteer? So you can meet cool people?" Samuel was watching Harold cut himself a couple of squares of Auntie Sadie's baked bannock. After Harold was finished with the knife, he handed it off to his little cousin.

"I *am* the cool people, little cousin!" Harold snapped his fingers. "Nah. I like meeting awesome people, but it's not about that. There's a lot of poor people in the city. It's a pretty stark environment if you don't have the cash to go to its better bits. Everyone needs music." Harold smiled and spread jam on buttered bannock.

Chickadee dug around in Auntie Sadie's refrigerator. She grabbed a package of sliced vegetables from the fridge and moved to the doorway to get out the way of the feeding frenzy.

Otter took the popcorn out of the cupboard and placed it on the counter. Atim grabbed it and tried to pour the popcorn into the hot air popper. Looking down, his long bangs fell in his eyes. As Atim tried to flick his vision clear, his movement sent an army of kernels scattering over the floor. Quickly, he crouched down to corral the fleeing yellow orbs. As Samuel stepped back from cutting his bannock, a kernel bit into his heel. With a shout, he clutched his foot in pain. Otter smacked his forehead in consternation and stared up at the ceiling.

"Let's get out of here before the Three Stooges drag us in!" Harold pulled on Chickadee's sleeve and, with his bannock now jammed and plated, headed for the living room.

Chickadee shared a weak grin with her older cousin. Once they were on the couch with their snacks, Harold teased, "So, that was at least worth a chuckle, and all I got was a smile. What's wrong?" He leaned over and gave her a nudge.

"I want to talk to Grandpa." Chickadee sighed and took a bite of a carrot.

"Wow! He doesn't have a phone. How do you call him on the rez?" Harold stared into the distance, trying to figure out how to solve the challenge.

"I've never had to call him on the rez." Chickadee laughed.

"Well…when my mom wants to talk to him…" Harold rubbed his jaw as he thought, "she calls your mom. And then you run down the hill and tell Grandpa that my mom wants to talk to him. A day or two later, he finds a phone, and calls back."

"Mmm…I think there's something wrong with that plan," Chickadee deadpanned.

"Well…didn't one of our cousins back on the rez, I think it was Mark, tell me he got an iPad for Christmas?" Harold squinted at Chickadee as he tried to squeeze out the memory.

"Yes! We were watching videos on it at the House-teraunt!" Chickadee pointed her finger skyward.

"I'm going to use FaceTime, call Mark, and see where he's at." Harold whipped out his cell.

The whirr and blow of the hot air popper could be heard from the kitchen. "Sounds like those boneheads have figured out how to pop popcorn." Harold laughed as he waited for his cousin Mark to answer. Eventually, they heard the triple tone that meant someone had answered their FaceTime phone call.

A brief jog by Mark and forty-five minutes later, Chickadee was looking at Grandpa through Harold's phone. The boys screamed, "Hello!" at Grandpa as they watched the movie. Chickadee took the small tablet into the empty basement.

"How are you doing, Grandpa?" Chickadee smiled into the screen.

"Can you see me, Chickadee? Can you see me?" Grandpa shouted.

"I can hear you, Grandpa. I'm far away, but the micro-phone is close." Chickadee giggled.

"Are you teasing me?" Grandpa said, quieter and serious.

"Yes, Grandpa." Chickadee smiled behind her hand.

Grandpa giggled. "Why am I standing in my back-yard, little one?" As Grandpa looked around, he panned the camera. Chickadee could see that he was indeed standing behind his house.

"Because you're borrowing the Ferland's WiFi, Grandpa." Chickadee didn't want to have to explain all that to her Elder, so she changed the subject quickly. "I'm sorry, Grandpa, but we didn't find your sister." Her voice cracked a little as she said it. The emotion came up quickly and she couldn't hold it back. She covered her face as the tears began to flow.

"It's okay, little one. It's okay. I shouldn't have put so much on you. I should have known you would take it to your heart." Grandpa held his screen close to his face.

"I'm fine. I'm just upset about a bunch of things. We did find some stuff." Chickadee went on to explain how they had tracked down Auntie Charlotte's picture, her date of birth, and her file at the provincial adoption registrar. "But then, we hit a wall," Chickadee explained. "We have some papers for you to fill out. If she's looking for us, then maybe we could connect."

"Well, it's amazing how much you've learned. I will fill them out, as soon as you bring them," Grandpa promised.

"Okay, Grandpa." Chickadee smiled sadly at her Elder.

"Little one, is there something else that is bothering you?" Grandpa looked concerned.

"It's just…" she sobbed. "This trip, there was so much to see…and so much that happened…."

"Not all of it good?" Grandpa asked.

"Not all of it good," Chickadee confirmed. "And now, I'm just tired."

"It's okay. I understand. The city is an amazing thing, but it moves very fast."

"It changes people." Chickadee pictured Brett as she said it.

"It does. You are the land you live on." Grandpa chuckled. "The city is built for humans, and so it is the perfect nest for people. But that also means its dark places, its failings, its cracks are made for humans as well." Grandpa stared off screen, lost in thought.

"A friend of ours, well, he used to be a friend..." Chickadee's lip began to quiver.

"He got lost?" Grandpa spoke after it was clear she couldn't.

Chickadee nodded.

"Funny thing about the city. We have pushed out all the big souls." Grandpa's face left the screen as he laughed. "The animal brothers in the city are the domesticated, the scavengers, or the frightened. Have you seen the news stories when a moose or even a little deer wanders into the city? Not all souls are allowed there. Even the gentle spirit of the deer causes chaos."

"Why is that, Grandpa?"

"My brother grew up with me, eating a lot of wild food that was butchered at home. I remember my brother telling me once, when he moved to the city, he got his chicken all clean, on a Styrofoam plate, with the bone, fat, and veins all cut away. Nice, white meat all the time. He got used to it. He said his first taste of good ol' duck soup back home was a surprise. Especially, with all the skin and bones and legs thrown in for people to pick at." Grandpa laughed at his brother again, as he probably had many times before. "He grew up on duck soup. And then, all of a sudden, it was…icky."

Chickadee was suddenly looking at a blur, then Grandpa's leg, then another blur, then the sky, all while listening to her Grandpa laugh. Chickadee giggled herself.

"Grandpa! Grandpa!" she shouted at Harold's phone. Eventually, the old man's wrinkled face once again filled the screen.

"Good thing they didn't serve moose nose." Grandpa guffawed a few more times and then took control of himself.

"Thanks for making me feel better, Grandpa. I was feeling…a little lost myself." Chickadee kissed her hand and then pressed it to the screen.

"You'll be home soon, little one. And then, it will be easier to make you smile." Grandpa waved at her as he held the screen at arm's length. Then suddenly there was a blur, her Elder's leg going back and forth, and then Grandpa's voice. "Mark! Mark! How do I shut this thing off?!"

Chickadee smiled and sighed.

CHAPTER 25
Quest Continued

She was in a room she didn't recognize. The smell of dust was almost overwhelming. She coughed. The bed was shabby. The blankets were threadbare and worn. There was little furniture; a bed, a three-drawer dresser, and a tiny nightstand. She opened a dark, wood door that led down a long hall. The bedrooms were empty of life, but full of furniture and evidence of habitation. She called out. No reply. The living room looked like a showroom in a catalogue. The rest of the house was in much better shape than her drab space. She walked through a kitchen, empty but for tiled counters, long-legged stools, and the hum of a fridge. Eventually, a utility room with a washer and dryer, and the back door. She tried the doorknob. Locked. She wanted to get out. It was an itch in her spine. There was something wrong in this house. She hurried back to the living room. Dust fell like a soft snow on every surface. It filled her with fear. She had to get it off.

A feather duster was in hand. Frantically, she tried to sweep away the ever-thickening powder. Her fear increased with the dust. She coughed, gagged. She had to get out. She ran to the front door. Turning the knob produced no results. She pulled and pulled, but the thick, wood door refused to open. Fear rose so high it threatened to overwhelm. She went to a front window. Two boys were working out in the yard. She couldn't let them see her. She couldn't. She ran to the back door. It refused to budge. She looked out the back window. Atim, Samuel, and Otter stood in a small city park. She called out to her boys. "I'm here! I'm here!" They didn't react. She pounded on the windows. The boys seemed to be wait-ing, but they obviously couldn't hear her increasingly frantic pleas. She banged harder on the windows. "I'm here!"

To her surprise, Chickadee came into view.

"That's not me!" Chickadee realized she was dreaming. Suddenly, she was standing on the sidewalk.

"I'm here!" The cry echoed within her. She looked up, the brown, black, and gray of the adoption registry building stretched up into the sky.

★

"Hey! Hey! Chickadee. You okay?" Samuel was staring down at her, concerned.

Chickadee waved him away and worked to sit up. "What?"

"You were yelling in your sleep." Otter looked worried. "What did I say?"

"'I'm here,' I think." Atim leaned over the bed.

Chickadee looked around. The morning sun was streaming through the windows. The other Muskrats were so serious. Suddenly, she waved her arms in the air excitedly and screamed, "Help! I'm still here! I'm still here! Someone wake me up!"

The boys fell over laughing.

After the Muskrats finished giggling, Sam was still curious. "No really, what were you dreaming about?"

"Auntie Charlotte, I think. She's here…still. She wants us to go back." Chickadee sometimes wasn't sure what her dreams meant, but as she said this, her heart was certain.

"Go back?" Atim wiped his sleepy eyes.

"Go back to the adoption registry with the forms." A plan was coming together in Chickadee's mind. "We need to get Auntie Sadie to sign them."

"I thought Grandpa was supposed to do it." Otter got off the fold-out and began to search the floor for cleanish clothes. The other boys did the same.

"Let's ask her, she can look at the papers and let us know if she can do it. Cool?" Chickadee bartered.

"You know, I kinda wanted to go to the mall." Atim smelled a sock.

"Today is our last day here. If we do it through snail mail, it will take weeks. This way, we could take Grandpa an answer tomorrow." Chickadee's voice held a twinge of annoyance.

Atim sighed. "Well! If it'll help Grandpa find his sister...I can't think of anything else I'd like to do in the city."

"I think we need to close the circle on this...." Chickadee nodded at her cousins.

The Mighty Muskrats were off to find their final clue.

CHAPTER 26

A Final Journey

"We have to stop meeting like this!" Atim held his arms out wide as he walked through the door of the provincial adoption agency.

Janice was already at the counter. She smiled as she put down the paperwork she was working on. "I thought I was rid of you." She stepped back as the Muskrats' elbows spread over the counter.

Chickadee slapped the signed paperwork down. "We brought it, Janice! Can we get any info now?" She smiled, brightly.

"You're not going to hold us up in red tape, are ya, Janice?" Sam teased.

Janice shook her head. It was obvious the Muskrats had reached a new comfort level with her. She held out her hand. "Let me see." She scanned the paperwork with her finger.

As she read, Janice took out a large, steel stamp from a shelf under the counter, then carefully placed an ink pad beside it. "Looks like it is all here." Her eyes crinkled as she grinned. With a flourish, she grabbed the stamp, plunged it into the ink pad, and then forcefully brought it down on the form. She studied the stamp on the paper and, once satisfied, tossed it over her shoulder. The Muskrats cheered.

"Mrs. Yenna isn't here, obviously," Janice faux whispered as she hid her mouth from a non-existing listener. "Easy to be brave."

The Muskrats laughed.

"Okay. How can you help us?" Atim tapped the back of the computer screen.

"Of course, Mr. All-business." She looked at Atim from the edge of her eye as she took the chair behind the computer. "I was looking at her file earlier. I did another search for students from Windy Lake, crossed with paperwork that started in Alberta. I got a new name, Joan Stewart. Stewart is the surname of the older lady who first adopted her."

"Really?" Chickadee leaned in.

"Eventually, she was given to Mrs. Stewart's daughter. She owned a farm, had two boys of her own, and a husband. But Joan started running away. So, she was adopted by another family, the Bauman's. Joan, I mean Charlotte, lived there for a few years, but started running away again.

It looks like her file was closed shortly after she turned sixteen."

"At sixteen? Why then?" Samuel spoke over the passing rumble of a bus.

"Not sure." Janice shrugged. "But fifty years ago, there were girls getting married at sixteen. If she married, she'd be considered an adult."

"You wouldn't want to drive us to Alberta, would ya?" Atim smiled at Janice.

"I don't think we're going to learn anything else unless we go there." Samuel pinched his chin as he thought.

"There's nothing there that says she's looking for Grandpa?" Chickadee's voice was not quite squeezed of hope.

Janice looked at Chickadee and slowly shook her head. "There is no indication that she reached out, but there is an e-mail here, from a Christina Bauman." Janice grabbed the pad beside the computer and wrote out a name and an e-mail address.

"It's not her, but it's her adopted sister, maybe?" Chickadee's brow furrowed.

"Looks like." Janice nodded. "Not her, but someone from her second adopted family."

"Not good," Otter said, sadly.

"Why, Otter?" Atim asked in confusion, shrugging his shoulders.

"Because, it wouldn't be proper.... Unless, Aunt Charlotte couldn't do it herself."

Sam and Chickadee thought for a moment. And then their shoulders dropped.

After saying good-bye to Janice, they started back to the mall. The Muskrats walked in silence, each alone with their own thoughts.

After a few moments, Atim cleared his throat. "Uh… that means Auntie Charlotte is probably dead, right?"

Sadly, the rest of the Muskrats nodded their heads.

Atim shrunk. Samuel patted him on the shoulder in sympathy.

"We found her, then we lost her, and now we have to tell Grandpa."

CHAPTER 27

Heading Home

"There it is…." Chickadee looked out a backseat window at the city nestled in the haze of the distance. They were close enough that the suburbs lay like a field before them and the few tall buildings of downtown loomed large in the distance. But they were far enough away to be traveling at highway speeds, with trees and farmhouses, occasionally, blocking the view of the urban environment.

"We almost got to the Exhibition Fair." Atim harrumphed from the middle of the back seat.

From the front, Samuel turned to his brother. "On the positive side, we met a nice taxi driver who didn't let us get taken for a ride."

"I saw Wovoka's Wail in concert!" Otter said excitedly, then a little quieter, "Their guitarist, anyway."

"I guess, we could say we were roadies for a concert," Atim said.

"Paid in hot dogs," Samuel added.

The Muskrats all chuckled at themselves.

"It sounds like you've had a great trip." Auntie Maude took inventory as she settled into long-distance driving mode. The area around her seat was packed with snacks, liquids, and lotion wipes.

"It wasn't what I thought it would be. Some places are so empty, and some places are so full." Otter stared out his window at the countryside rolling by. He had no wish to look back at the city.

"It's dirty too," Chickadee said with disappointment.

They rode in silence through a few small towns.

"I remember once, I can't remember where I was coming back from, but I was dressed up. I had this nice dress on, high heels. But I was broke too, you know?" Auntie Maude laughed. "Probably a job interview or something."

"I know what rush hour is now!" Otter bragged.

"It's the only time Auntie Sadie swears!" Atim announced.

Auntie Maude laughed, then continued her story. "Well, I had no bus fare, so I was walking back, probably to my boyfriend's or my auntie's house. I needed to pee. I needed to pee bad. But all around me were office buildings. Eventually, I couldn't help it anymore, I went into one of the office buildings. I picked a government one because I thought they'd have to let me. But the security guard wouldn't allow me in. And the next one didn't either. That lady was so mean. I just needed to pee!" Auntie Maude slapped Samuel's arm beside her and then hid her laughter behind her hand.

"Were your teeth floating, Mom?" Atim tapped her shoulder.

"Oh yeah, my eyes were yellow. I got to a corner store, but they wouldn't let me go pee unless I bought something. None of the stores would. It hurt so bad." She shook her head. "As I walked down the street, I was thinking of all the pipes below me that ran from bathrooms. All the bathrooms around me. Even trees, that I would have no problem peeing behind if I was in the bush, but I couldn't because I was in the city. It wasn't like there wasn't any place built for peeing around me. All those pipes, all those toilets in the buildings, all those trees…" Aunt Maude trailed off.

"The whole landscape was built for urination is what you're saying, hey, Mom?" Samuel slapped his mother's arm.

She burst into laughter. The little van shook. She slapped the wheel and the van swerved.

Atim reach from the backseat and hit his brother. "Stop making Mom laugh! You're going to kill us!"

Auntie Maude had to stop laughing and catch her breath before she could speak again.

"Such a simple thing, a human bodily function, I was surrounded by toilets, but it was the people that were getting in the way. That's the city for you." Auntie Maude shrugged. "It's a funny place, the city. People think it's a destination. It isn't. It's another landscape filled with its own destinations. So many people I've known, who thought they were going to the city to get somewhere, never got to where they were going once they were there."

Chickadee was lost in thought about her auntie Charlotte and the mystery that had yet to be completed. She would head for the Muskrat clubhouse as soon as she could. She needed to e-mail a lady in Alberta.

CHAPTER 28

A Sister's Story

"Do I have to go in the backyard?" Grandpa sounded hurried for the first time anyone in the room could remember. He came bolting out of his bedroom armed with a mug of tea in one hand and a notepad in the other. He made a beeline for the front door.

"We'll watch it in your living room, Grandpa, if we're all in the backyard, the Ferland's will know the whole family is using their WiFi!" Otter and Atim stopped their Elder and turned him around. The boys had never seen Grandpa so excited.

"It's all hooked up?"

"Samuel is standing outside, Grandpa. With Mark's tablet. But we got a long cord. See?" Atim pointed to a thin, black cord that snaked from a window in Grandpa's guest room, down the hallway, and into the living room. As they walked in, a collection of family and friends welcomed Grandpa. A spot had been reserved for him right in front of the TV. Chickadee was already sitting on one side. Otter sat on the other. The old man fell into his spot with a plop.

With a loud creak, Grandpa's door swung open and a group of the older cousins spilled in. They laughed and joked as they kicked off their shoes.

Chickadee picked Denice out of the pack. She hopped off the couch and ran to her favorite older cousin.

"Hey, Denice!"

"Aww, Chickie. How you doin'? I heard you all got into some trouble in the city."

Everyone else in the new group continued on into the house. Chickadee and Denice stepped out of the doorway and leaned on the kitchen counter.

"So, what happened?" Denice smiled down at Chickadee.

"Ah, it's a long story, but we did some dumb stuff, and the boys got into even worse trouble, but then…we found Auntie Charlotte. Or, at least, we could tell Grandpa what happened to her."

"The Mighty Muskrats solved the case!" Denice lightly punched her on the shoulder. "The whole family is freaked out, seriously. I know Grandpa…well, you gave him something."

Chickadee tried to say something, but she just giggled and turned red instead.

Denice put one arm around her little cousin and squeezed. She then nodded toward the living room and started heading in.

When Chickadee saw the seat beside Grandpa was still open, she sat down, swung her arms wide, and clasped him in a bear hug. As she listened to her Grandpa's heartbeat, she remembered the e-mail that brought them all there.

After their trip to the city, each of the Muskrats had found a new appreciation for their hometown and some of its unique people and places. There was no rush hour here.

Chickadee remembered how she'd enjoyed the smells of the grass, soil, and pine as she watched the field and junkyard around the Muskrats' fort. The sun shone; the wind played with the edges of her long, black hair. It was quiet.

Soon after her arrival home, she'd walked to the old, blue Bombardier snow-van that was half-hidden in the collection of rusting cars, trucks, construction equipment, and metal that had been corralled in the small field. The vehicle had been a workhorse in the north back when Grandpa was a working man. Its large skis replaced front wheels in the winter and a half-track pushed it through the bush.

Chickadee opened the door of the Bombardier. Once inside, she looked out through its windows to see if anyone had seen her arrive.

The interior of the snow van was a pre-teen's dream. Cushions and blankets softened the harsh edges of the aging wood. Posters of pop stars were plastered in strategic locations between the windows. The magazines they were pulled from were neatly stacked in easy reach.

When she was sure she had arrived unseen, Chickadee slid her hand along a tin panel that had once hidden the engine area from the sitting and storage area. She smiled. The latch had already been undone, which probably meant one of the other Muskrats was inside. With a slight tug, she pulled the panel open, climbed in, and closed the panel behind her. The engine had been replaced with the end of an old culvert that led into the darkness. Boards and bits of carpet had been laid on the floor of the aluminum tunnel to make the kneeling journey a little less painful. The other end of the culvert was stuck in the rear emergency doorway of a decommissioned school bus.

The view out of the majority of the bus windows was the stacked vehicles in the junkyard. But here and there, a glimpse of the field beyond the mounds of steel could be seen. An overturned car sat on the front of the bus, with the windshield gone, it turned the hood into a large enclosed shelf.

"Tansi!" Otter said.

Chickadee stood after crawling through the long culvert. "I'm good. You?" Chickadee stretched her back.

"I was just…enjoying the quiet," Otter told her. He was reading a *Conan* comic as he sprawled across one of the couches along the long wall of the school bus.

Chickadee put on the manner of their grandfather. "Silence is the voice of Creation."

They both laughed.

"I came to check my e-mails." Chickadee was almost apologetic as she walked past him to the computer. She sat down and soon her fingers were like tap-dancing spiders across the keyboard. "Grandpa gave me permission to e-mail the woman from Alberta. I asked her if she would FaceTime with Grandpa and tell him the story of his little sister."

"Yeah. It still blows me away that Grandpa doesn't know anything about someone he loved so much. Imagine being taken away from your family like that."

Chickadee had been excited to see a reply e-mail. She clicked on it quickly and read. "She'll do it!" Chickadee clapped her hands.

After a quick reply, it had taken a few weeks to arrange a time in the summer when Ms. Bauman could video chat with Grandpa. But, eventually, the date was set, and the family was invited and assigned food to bring.

★

Now, a parade of children running over Chickadee's feet ripped away the memory. As the little hoard of attention-seeking and killer-cuteness peaked and ebbed, the sitting adults and teens returned to their conversations.

From outside, she could hear Samuel screaming, "Is everyone ready?"

A chorus of "Aho!" from the men and "Get on with it!" from the women, went up. The family turned to the TV.

Chickadee could feel her hand squeezed tightly in the warm, silky grasp of her grandpa. He was trembling with excitement. The whole family had been concerned about Grandpa's health after he first learned his little sister had passed on.

Sam's face popped up on the TV screen. Everyone in the living room screamed and clapped.

"Hey! I saw this one. Change the channel!" one of the cousins yelled.

"Okay! I'll call her up." Samuel's face was replaced by the logo of FaceTime.

Eventually, a woman's kind face filled the screen. She had a toothy smile that was welcoming and warm. Her hair was gray with wisps of auburn. Her skin, clear with the occasional freckle, was crinkled and tanned like she had spent much of her long life outdoors. Her eyes were shy, but her smile lines suggested she had spent a lifetime pushing herself past her fear of strangers.

"Hello! You look a little young to be Charlotte's brother!" The lady chuckled.

"I'm her brother!" Grandpa yelled to the screen in the living room.

"She can't hear you!" Otter whispered to his Elder. "Our camera is on the tablet in the backyard, Grandpa." Otter tapped his Elder on the leg.

From the backyard, and on the little square at the corner of the TV, Samuel spoke.

"What? Oh!" he said. "I'm Sam. I'll be your host this evening. My grandpa is in his living room, watching you on his TV screen. His grandchildren will relay the messages back and forth. We have to do it like this because my grandpa doesn't have Internet."

"Okay! Well, I hope to meet him one day," the lady said pleasantly. "I don't know how to start here. I…I'm Joan's sister. I guess that sounds odd." She shook her head and struggled on. "I'm told you knew her as Charlotte. That's a lovely name. When Joan…Charlotte…was with our family, things were good for her. I loved her. I don't know what you know. I don't know what I can tell you. What do you want to know?"

"Ask Grandpa what he wants to know!" Samuel motioned to Atim, whose athletic form went running into the house. He returned a moment later.

"He said, 'How did she pass?'" Atim looked serious.

Sam relayed the question gently.

"Oh. Well, she died of cancer. Last summer. It was very fast. She was never…robust, you know. She was so thin when I first met her. I remember…I guess, that is the beginning, I should start there, I suppose." Christina Bauman looked off-screen as she remembered.

"I was at Sunday school—I was only a little girl—when I heard two ladies from my church talking. One of them was a recent widow, Mrs. Stewart. She was having difficulty keeping her property and doing all the stuff it took to keep a home in those days. The other lady said, 'Why don't you get a boy?'" Christina paused again, re-membering. "So strange to realize now, that…I guess they just knew there was this…collection of children that they could go look at. And then…just take one."

Samuel shifted uncomfortably. Atim's eyebrows got higher and higher as he listened to the lady's story.

After a moment's pause, Christina began again.

"It was a few months later that Joan first arrived. I had no idea Mrs. Stewart renamed her. I felt for Joan. She worked so hard for Mrs. Stewart. And the old lady treated her like she was a servant, not a child." Christina shook her head.

"It only got worse when Mrs. Stewart died. I guess, she was inherited by Mrs. Stewart's daughter. I don't remem-ber her married name, but we always called her Tabby."

Christina sighed heavily. "Tabby had two boys. Joan couldn't even escape that family at school. She was expected to serve those boys everywhere. I don't know everything that happened in that house but I watched Joan get quieter and quieter, more and more shy."

Christina sobbed, suddenly. She reached off-screen for some tissue and dabbed her eyes and cheeks. "I'm sorry. I miss her. She didn't deserve…"

Samuel motioned to Atim and hissed, "Go see how Grandpa is doing."

Atim ran into the house. His eyes had to adjust from sunlight to the darker house. The family was deathly quiet. Some of the aunties wiped tears from their faces. Atim looked at Grandpa and his heart fell.

The old man was sitting on the edge of the couch, tears openly trailed down his cracked, brown cheeks. He desperately clasped Otter's hand on one side and Chickadee's on the other.

Atim knew that Grandpa's arms might be thin with age, but they held a sinewy strength that was now squeezing his cousins' hands tightly. They both looked at Atim with a gaze filled with the weight of their Elder's sorrow.

On the TV, Christina sobbed, wiping tears from her face. Atim ran back outside.

"Joan…Charlotte…was such a beautiful soul. Her life had been so hard, you know. I guess you *don't* know. But her life had been hard, yet…she carried herself with strength."

Christina tried to rein in her emotions. She blew her nose into a tissue. "I loved her so much. She was my sister…. I hope that doesn't offend. I just…when Jo—Charlotte—began to run away from Tabby's, I heard my mother talking about it. I was a teenager by this time. I begged my mom to see if we could take her in. And then…we did. Charlotte was so gentle, so kind. It took us a long time to convince her that we loved her. That we didn't just want her there as a servant. It was wonderful to finally have a sister."

The lady from Alberta sobbed again, and tears dropped from her cheeks.

"We're sorry to make you go through this, Ms. Bauman," Samuel said.

Christina smiled a sad smile that took over her whole face. She shook her head.

Atim took the pause as a chance to run into the house. The scene was as before. Weeping aunties, Grandpa on the edge of his seat, Ms. Bauman's face on the television.

"It's okay. This is good. Kind of healing, you know," Christina said. "She…wanted to find her family but, I don't know, she was frightened of what she'd find, or maybe she was scared she'd be rejected."

Before Samuel could say anything, Christina began to speak again. "I tried so hard to convince her that she wasn't lost!"

She looked earnestly into the camera, shaking slightly. "But I couldn't. She began to run away again. When she left home, she was so hungry for love. She always had a boyfriend, if he was a good man, her life was good. But several were not good men. Her heart was sick…sick with sadness, I guess."

Inside the house, Grandpa seemed to shrink.

Chickadee squeezed her Elder's hand. "We can stop, Grandpa!" Her eyes filled with tears as she watched the pain in his face.

"No!" Grandpa suddenly tried to stand up. Chickadee and Otter helped him rise. He indicated he wanted to head toward the door, so Chickadee stepped back.

"This is good. For both of us." Grandpa moved quickly to the entrance. The determined leader in him was back. The family made a path for their Elder, Otter, and Chickadee. They followed Grandpa as he walked outside in his hide slippers. Once in the backyard, he looked around for Samuel, found him, and made a beeline for the tablet.

"Let me see her." Grandpa held out his hand. Samuel handed him the screen. The family gathered around their Elder and the Muskrats.

Grandpa sighed. And then he turned the tablet to his face and looked into the eyes of the lady in Alberta.

"Hello, Ms. Bauman. I am Charlotte's older brother. I…I want to thank you…for loving her. For being there when we could not be there." Grandpa stopped, obviously, trying to maintain control. His eyes filled to the brim with tears, but they did not spill over.

Christina covered her mouth with her hand and began to cry again. "I'm sorry...." Her shoulders shook.

"Do not be sorry. You showed her love. They took her from us. They gave her to people who did not love her..." Grandpa shook his head. "When her path crossed yours, you did what you could to help her, not for what she could do for you, but because she was a young girl who needed love. Thank you for that."

Ms. Bauman seemed slightly stronger. She smiled at Grandpa through the tears. "She was such a beautiful soul...." Her mouth twisted sadly. She almost started to cry again, but she straightened herself.

"She was." Grandpa smiled.

"I am so sorry for your loss." Christina's lips tightened for a moment, but she smiled again. "But...it looks like you have a lot of family to support you."

Grandpa looked around him at his adult children, their spouses, and his grandchildren.

"I do." He nodded at them all. His eyes finally fell on the Muskrats. He motioned to them. "Gather 'round me, Muskrats. Let's do a, what do you call it? A selfie."

Chickadee, Otter, Samuel, and Atim gathered around their Elder and looked into the camera.

"Can you see them?" Grandpa asked.

Otter pointed to the little square that showed their faces.

"Oh. There we are. I need longer arms." Grandpa chuckled. The Muskrats squeezed close to their Elder.

"See them?" Grandpa said proudly.

"I see them. Is that Chickadee?" Christina waved at them from the screen.

"These are the ones who brought you to me," Grandpa said proudly.

"Hello! Thank you, children." Ms. Bauman smiled at them.

"Our community calls them the Mighty Muskrats," Grandpa told her.

Ms. Bauman laughed. "Is that a good name?"

Grandpa and the rest of the family guffawed.

"I think someone was trying to be funny when they gave them that one." Grandpa looked at each of the Muskrats in turn. "But I think it is a good name. The muskrat fed us when bigger game was scarce. Its fur kept us warm. Back in the old days, the muskrat was like our macaroni-and-cheese—easy to prepare comfort food."

Grandpa beamed at the lady in Alberta. "Humble though it was, the muskrat helped us through the tough times. And these ones…" he playfully shook Otter in a one-armed hug, "…these ones found my lost sister. These little Muskrats helped me close a hole in my heart. They brought us you, Charlotte's sister. And now, it looks like the Muskrats have a new auntie."

Ms. Bauman covered her mouth, took a deep breath, held it, and then let it out slowly.

"I…would be honored to be a part of Charlotte's

family. I would love to get to know you all better." Ms. Bauman's smile seemed to shine right from her heart.

"Hey!" Mr. Ferland was on his back porch, looking over at the family. "What are you guys all doing in the backyard?"

A chorus of "Oh!" "Eyee-ahh!" and "Oh, heck!" went up from the family, and they all turned and started heading back to the house.

"Remember, we're...uh...borrowing the Ferland's WiFi, Grandpa!" Sam whispered in his Elder's ear.

Grandpa's eyebrows shot up. He looked at Ms. Bauman. "Welcome to the family! Chickadee will e-mail you! We've got to go now!" Grandpa gave a quick smile and then handed the tablet to Samuel.

Ms. Bauman put up a weak protest to Grandpa leaving. The screen was starting to freeze in quick blinks.

"Sorry, Ms. Bauman! Our...the WiFi signal is getting weak. Chickadee will e-mail you!" Sam yelled.

The screen went black. Samuel was suddenly looking at the FaceTime call disconnected page. He unplugged the cord that led through the window to the television and caught up to the other Muskrats helping their Elder into the house.

Grandpa's door gave its customary complaint as they entered. On the inside, the family had all stopped and turned, now forming a gauntlet of congratulations and kudos. The uncles slapped the Muskrats on the back and the aunties embraced them as they followed the family patriarch. Denice hugged them all roughly. Everyone was happy to know about Auntie Charlotte. She had gone on her final journey, but it was obvious that she was still a part of the family.

At the end of the line, Grandpa turned and gave the four of them a big hug. His smile was legendary. Their hearts were bursting with love and pride. When he let them go, their Elder kept them close and whispered, "Little ones, you found out what happened to my lost sister…and you brought me a new one. Thank you. Thank you, my Mighty Muskrats."

Epilogue

"Make sure those are healthy Grandfathers before you put them on the fire!"

Grandpa yelled the caution at Mark and Otter in the distance as they picked through a pile of rocks for ones suitable for heating within the steam-filled sweat lodge. The stones had to be the right kind, strong enough not to crack in the fire or burst when water was poured over them. Many First Nations called such stones "grandfathers" as a show of respect for the sweat lodge and its teachings.

Not so far away, Atim and Samuel cut wood and kindling for an extended fire. Chickadee was preparing the picnic table area outside the Cultural Camp's kitchen where the feast was being prepared. The plywood building was painted red and rested on cinder blocks. It was one of the few roofed buildings among the many family teepees.

"I want everything to be ready for my sisters." Grandpa smiled as he brought out tablecloths from the kitchen.

"It's good of you to bring Ms. Bauman into the family." Chickadee used a stick to remove a blackened kettle from over the cooking fire. She placed it on a counter that had been built along the outside kitchen wall. With a cloth to protect her hand from the heat, she poured the hot water over a tea bag in a large mug, and then put it on the picnic table near her grandfather. The old man sat on the bench but didn't put his legs under the table.

"She was my sister's sister. And she has told me that she also dreams of Charlotte, like you, little one." Grandpa spooned a touch of sugar into his tea.

"Yeah, I still dream of her. It's like she is calling to me. It can be emotional sometimes." Chickadee spoke quietly as she looked at her feet.

"It is time for the both of you to let her go." Grandpa shrugged. "She needed to speak loudly to connect you two, but now, we are all coming together. Her work on this earth is done, but she is still echoing in both your hearts. All of you must go your separate ways. You will come into the sweat with us."

"The sweat? Really?" Chickadee was happily surprised. In her family, a girl's first sweat was usually during her Mother Bear teachings, the lessons the family Grandmothers taught her when she reached womanhood.

"It's important for you and Ms. Bauman to sweat together and you can sing your auntie Charlotte along on her next journey. It is obvious she has chosen to be a helper for the family from the other side, but it is time for you both to let her go." Grandpa took a sip of his tea.

"This is all so strange, Grandpa. How we lost her. How we found her. Why did they take her in the first place, Grandpa?"

"Because they are the land they live on." Grandpa smiled. "The city tells its people a story like all landscapes. But the story of the city is the story of man, not Mother Earth. The ant in the anthill never forgets that it is one for all, but the man in the city is easily convinced it is all for one. And when it is all for one, there is no room for others."

"But the city people say they're just trying to make a better life for themselves. Isn't that what we're all supposed to be doing?" Chickadee really wanted to understand where the colonialists went wrong in how they treated her people.

"Do you think the Sacred Teachings like Respect and Kindness are just nice ways to treat each other?" Grandpa smiled at Chickadee when a look of surprise crossed her face. "Yesterday, today, and tomorrow, they are laws of nature. If these laws are broken, it creates an imbalance, a loss of center. Do you understand?"

Chickadee nodded, and Grandpa continued.

"It's good to build a better life for your children. But you must always respect others' rights to build a better life for *their* children. To do that, they must have their own languages, laws, and lands. That is where the English, the French, and Canada went wrong. When they took away our ability to live our cultures and teach them to our children, the Settlers strayed from the right path. When the city people wanted to control our way of life, First Nations children—our brothers and sisters and cousins—paid the price."

"And Auntie Charlotte?"

"And, yes, my little sister, Charlotte. It will take me a lifetime to heal. I passed my pain down to my children, I know I did. It will take some time for our family to find balance."

"Can I do anything, Grandpa? To help us heal?"

"A good start would be making sure that you and your children can one day speak to their Elders in Cree. Understand our teachings, our laws, in our own languages."

"Will the city people support that?" Chickadee wondered out loud.

Grandpa shook his head. "I'm not sure, but both First Nations and Canadians need a lot of healing. All I know? The road signs to reconciliation around Windy Lake better be written in Cree." Grandpa laughed and slapped his granddaughter's shoulder. Chickadee giggled.

A snap and crackle through the trees told them a

car was about to turn off the gravel road. Grandpa and Chickadee watched as a small SUV pulled into the driveway. The other Muskrats stopped what they were doing and joined them. As the vehicle bounced over the muddy path, Grandpa and the Muskrats could see that Christina Bauman had finally arrived from Alberta.

"There is a lot to do to repair the relationship. But Charlotte has brought us someone she loved. Right?"

The Mighty Muskrats smiled at their Elder and nodded enthusiastically. Grandpa smiled back and then turned toward his guest.

"Okay, let's go meet your new auntie, Christina."

ABOUT THE AUTHOR

MICHAEL HUTCHINSON is a citizen of the Misipawistik Cree Nation in the Treaty 5 territory, north of Winnipeg. As a teen, he pulled nets on Lake Winnipeg, fought forest fires in the Canadian Shield, and worked at the Whiteshell Nuclear Research Station's Underground Research Lab. As a young adult, he worked as a bartender, a caterer for rock concerts and movie shoots, and, eventually, as a print reporter for publications such as *The Calgary Straight* and *Aboriginal Times*. After being headhunted by the Indian Claims Commission, Michael moved from journalism to the communications side of the desk and worked for the ICC in Ottawa as a writer. He returned to his home province to start a family. Since then, he has worked as the Director of Communications for the Assembly of Manitoba Chiefs, and as a project manager for the Treaty Relations Commission of Manitoba, where he helped create the "We are all treaty people" campaign. Over seven years ago, he jumped at the chance to make mini-documentaries for the first season of *APTN Investigates*. Michael then became host of APTN National News and produced APTN's sit-down interview show, *Face to Face*, and APTN's version of *Politically Incorrect*, *The Laughing Drum*. Michael was recently in charge of communications for the Manitoba Keewatinowi Okimakanak, an advocacy organization for First Nations in northern Manitoba. He currently lives in Ottawa, Ontario where he continues to advocate for First Nation families and communities across Canada. His greatest accomplishments are his two lovely daughters.